CRYPTOGRAM

David Michael Medina

authorHOUSE®

AuthorHouse™
1663 Liberty Drive
Bloomington, IN 47403
www.authorhouse.com
Phone: 1 (800) 839-8640

Published by AuthorHouse 03/07/2019

ISBN: 978-1-7283-0326-0 (sc)
ISBN: 978-1-7283-0325-3 (e)

Library of Congress Control Number: 2019902688

Print information available on the last page.

This book is printed on acid-free paper.

ONE DAY A LETTER ARRIVED IN THE MAIL... AND THEN SHE FREAKED!

Natalie Walker was devastated when it came to mind that she was no daughter of hers... The stupid step parents fault!

Then one day during Spring Break she got a letter that said that she was adopted and her parents were unknown citizens.

And she found out that she has a sibling.

She locked herself away in her bedroom and cried herself to sleep. She screamed for hours until her voice was gone.

And then she disappears one day, and they never saw her again until one night only......

THEN THE TERROR BEGINS!

CHAPTER 1

A perpetrator stands before a tall two story house located in a pleasant suburban neighborhood. The streets aligned with a dozen pink houses on both sides. The streets are slicked with fallen rain drops. The dark green grass is swollen with little bits of droplets. And the rainwater sizzled against the dash of a new Ford pick up.

One bedroom light is on upstairs.

The perpetrator heads for the front door and pried it open.

The sneaky stranger heads for the kitchen and finds a butcher knife and then heads for the upstairs hallway.

No need to turn the lights on. There are plenty of lightning in the evening sky to keep the place lit.

Amanda and her boyfriend Ray lay in bed all the while until the alarm on her cellphone came on at 11:00 PM.

Amanda got up fast, half naked in a satin robe, and began tying her hair back in a loop, and fixing it up with strings and tied knots, and everything.

Ray is still snoozing, laying dressed in his underwear, sound asleep, unafraid of what's about to happen tonight! Then...

All of a sudden Ray stands up in surprise.

"Having a bad dream?" Mandy asked.

"What the hell time is it?" Ray groaned.

"It's time to get up. My parents will be back soon," she said.

Ray snoozes soundly.

"Ray! Don't fall asleep."

"Hmmmm?" He moans.

"Ya' hear me? I said get up!" She screams.

Ray sits up.

"It's almost time. Eleven o'clock, now move over!" Mandy yells.

Ray sarcastically gleams at her, "Oooo, it's an emergency. Great... I'm up."

"Get dressed and be gone. If dad catches you here he'll scrub your face off with his ball catcher."

"Same time tomorrow, babe?" Ray asked, full of hope.

Amanda snoots at him, "Nope! And don't call me babe." She walks to the bathroom and bumps the door closed with the side of her hip.

"What's the problem?"

"You still being here, that's what the problem is!" She yelled from behind the closed door,

Ray whispers, "I don't need this shit." As he leaves, "I'll see ya'!" With a snobbish gesture and, tone.

"Mmm hmmm...." Mandy remarks low, and calm with empathy instead of sarcasm. Her usual too dark for me tone of voice. "Hahhhh," Amanda sighed, and calmly closes the shower curtains and began to unravel in thoughts and mystic aweness, as the shower curtain goes on, the gown clothes come off, and next comes down the cold shower water, rinsing away guilt, fear, and doubt.

Ray storms out from the master bedroom and through the hallway, looking mad as he please. He heard a loud "SLAM" like a cabinet door closing. At the top of the staircase, Ray stands in the dark, unaware of what's happening here.

Lightning flashes across the sky, brightening the corridor through the bedroom windows. And suddenly...

"What the f--------"

Ray is smacked in the face with a ten iron golf club. Blood sprays out of his forehead. And then he falls to the carpeted steps.

"Amanda!" Ray screams.

The intruder with the golf club interacts with a whooping and more.

Ray is smacked five more times with the awful golf club.

The noise of the shower drowns away the background noise coming from Ray and the stranger. Amanda showers during his brutal death.

Amanda continued showering while the dark intruder here takes Ray downstairs, dragging him by a foot, leaving blood puddles here and there.

The intruder takes Ray, half dead, down into the backyard and props him up on a summertime lawn chair, and does a few quick slashes with a knife. And gets to work on his balls with the sharp knife.

After Amanda showers, she blow dries her hair, leaving it hanging and long down past her shoulders,

She dresses into a night gown and slips away.

She walks through the upstairs hallway, the window behind her back flashes with lightening making her jump, and freeze. Then the sound of thunder hit. She gasps and, she continues walking down the hall.

"Daddy? What's going on? Was that you?" Amanda called down from upstairs.

She peers down from the corridor.

And next she walks downstairs and finds the trail of blood. She happened to notice it by stepping in it. Blood on the bottom of her feet.

She walks through the kitchen and out into the patio outside, near the backyard swimming pool area was. The lights are on.

Ray is propped up in a chair with his back turned.

"Ray!" she screamed. "What are you still doing here?"

She approaches Ray.

She yells again, "What are you doing? I said we're through for tonight!"

She steps an inch closer.

"Did you hear what I said?" She continued to freak out.

Amanda "Mandy" taps Ray's shoulder and discovers him dead, with his throat gashed out, face beaten, and both hands clutching down his bleeding groin. She gasps and panics. And then turns around and almost falls down into the swimming pool, then discovers Ray's penis floating in the pool. She cringes and almost pukes.

She slowly backs away from the pool and bumps into the silent perpetrator. Amanda turns around and runs into the killer who was also holding the knife that was used to conduct the killing. And its deep blade slit right into Amanda's belly.

That part was on accident. The killer meant no harm to Amanda.

Amanda whispers, "I never meant to hurt anyone. I don't want to die this way, I never will leave you, now."

Blood drips on the pavement between their feet.

Amanda falls backward into the swimming pool. Her arms wide open. Her bleeding tummy turning the pool water red, black, and green.

And the killer just stands there next to the swimming pool, looking down at the floating corpse of Amanda Reyes.

The killers eyes, cold angry, and gleaming.

The two bodies were discovered by Amanda's parents, they called the police, the bodies were collected, questions were asked, and the brutal words were, "Don't know how this happened."

The investigation began shortly thereafter.

A helicopter held up in the sky, a spotlight spread over the neighbors dream homes, the yard was lined with a yellow ribbon that said: SCENE OF A CRIME, DO NOT ENTER.

And policemen and coroners tour their way through in and throughout the house.

They took samples of blood and fingerprints from all of the scattered remains throughout the home.

In the backyard, Detective Lamar, late 50's, Latino/Caucasian American, stands there at the edge of the pool, looking down at the blood tainted water.

He peers off to the side at one of the paramedics, zipping the body bag closed, inside it was Amanda.

Lamar was notified by Officer Henry about a stolen vehicle. Amanda's car. A Buick.

License plate ripped off. A crack in it's windshield.

Then the officer produced a cryptic note made with scratch paper, and letters clipped from magazines and newspapers that told him: LET HER GO!

Lamar is called upon by his detective friend Tate. He asks for his assistance. Something to do with people in the yard up the street who know now who rescued the plant in the garbage can out front.

They have seen something fishy about the yard waste out front. Someone had to have wanted a better explanation than just two dead people yet to be.

A day later, the undertaker Robert Kimball, had finished examining the two dead bodies. Eric had just dropped by after he finished thorough labs done on Ray Larson's corpse.

The undertaker Robert tells Eric, "The girl drowned, and bled to death soon after she had been stabbed and dropped to zero temperature just before the medics arrived here. And it's obvious Ray took a beating. Three major organs carved right out of his body."

"Both of them dead with the same blade? A kitchen knife, perhaps," told Eric Lamar.

"Take a look here," Robert eyed the cadavers with sprintful behavior. "Took the two out with a bloody knife bath right here. It's nowhere near as possible as it turns out yet, here."

Robert drops the plastic bag with the knife in it onto the table next to Amanda's corpse.

Eric uses a meter reader to examine the edges of the blade.

"Mean!" Eric said. "Violent."

Robert continued, "We've got more come. The blood coming from the girls stab wound has a mix of one other blood type."

"That would be to be a residue left by the boy she was with. The killer used a single knife to kill both of them," Eric shrieks.

"The Reyes girl was with child. She was two months pregnant. The stab wound went through the unborn fetus as well," Robert Kimball declares.

"Ray Larson could not have been the father," Eric supposes.

"Are you sure?" Robert asked.

"Friends and families of the two murder victims all say that Amanda and Ray only met each other for the first time two days ago." Eric sighs, "two of them had multiple affairs," he gasps. "Can you run a DNA test on these two, and find out who the father is?"

"Certainly," Robert said.

CHAPTER 2

On a hot summer afternoon, Detective Eric Lamar stands before Lance's house, who was just about to load up the van to go hiking up in the mountains for the weekend. Fishing, bathing, and sunshine.

"Mister Lance Weston, how are ya'," said Detective Eric Lamar.

Lance turns around, eyes squinting in the sun, panting, mouth is dry, thirsty from the heat, "Yes, sir?"

"Detective Eric Lamar, homicide division."

Lance's father, early 60's, Caucasian, dressed in casual clothes, steps up, and stands near, right next to Lance. "Is there something wrong, Detective?"

"I'm investigating the murder of Amanda Reyes and Ray Larson, two of your former classmates and Will Wood High, is that correct?"

Lance frowned.

"How well did you know Amanda?" asked Lamar.

"I knew her during the beginning of Spring semester during my senior year," said Lance.

"It looks like you're planning on going somewhere. If you are leaving town for any particular reason, I must advise you not to," said Lamar.

Lance's father notices that there is a blonde woman standing down the street, next to the neighbor's yard picket fence, taking pictures of them.

Lance's father says, "Excuse me Detective Lamar, may we discuss this indoors?"

"Sure Mr. Weston," said the Detective. Before they went inside the house, Eric had noticed the blonde reporter down the street too.

Mr. Weston pours a few glasses of iced tea for Detective Lamar and Lance, seated at the guest room dining table.

"Thank you," Eric Lamar says, gently, almost a whisper. Takes a cube of sugar and drops it in his own glass, squeezes a lemon slice and stirs it gently into his tea and sighs, "I suppose you are wondering why you were one of our top choices on the suspect list. We have spoken to Amanda's cousins, friends, classmates, and relatives. Yes, there are a list of people who are involved suspect wise, everything from one night stands, co-workers at the mini mall to high school sweethearts and your name came up twice."

"What does this have to do with me?" Lance asks, slowly.

"The girl was two months pregnant when she was murdered. And you are the name that came up positive," Detective Lamar said exactly.

Lance sighs with discomfort.

"When did this happen, Detective Lamar?" Mr. Larson asks, scoldingly.

"Two nights ago, at her house. She was found dead with her boyfriend," said Lamar.

"Well I have not seen her in a month," said Lance. "And I was busy Friday night, sorry. I don't know who took the blame and killed her."

"Is that a fact, who were you with Friday night?" Eric said.

"Here with me and the wife. We spent half the night at the Baptist Church doing a wedding rehearsal for our daughter Brittany."

"Okay." Detective Lamar said. "Here is my card, if you hear anything, or see anyone strange, DO NOT hesitate to call me. I am going to pass your involvement to my partner Detective Stanley Tate. Stay close by until I tell you it's alright." Detective Lamar takes a slow sip from his glass. "Thanks for the tea. Excuse me."

Detective Tate steps into the kitchen at a random beat. A large, tall, black man, in his early 40's, dressed like an FBI professional, speaks in a more grim tone than Lamar, and questions for visibly. "Mr. Lance Weston, I am Detective Tate, it is a pleasure to meet you. Mind if I sit down?"

"Please do," said Lance.

"We are going to bring you down to the station and ask you some questions. It should take no longer than a half an hour. I hope you don't mind," Tates said.

Tate's impression he made on the young man loosened him up. Made him feel relaxed.

"All right," Lance said.

"It's going to be alright, son," said his father.

In the lobby at the police station, Lance seated in the guest room surrounded in suspects, other members of his Junior year classmates.

A Latina girl name Casey, clings closely to her boyfriend Jorge, eyeing Lance with a fierce crimson glare. Like Jorge, she wore urban gear street clothes, both she and her boyfriend wore the look of discomfort on their faces. They are here being questioned about some other girl they barely knew; makes them mad. And also, having their past mistakes brought up to the surface so quickly; makes them mad even more. They are pissed.

What's it going to be like when this is all over, Lance wondered.

Lance's tense eyes move at the girl and boy on the other side of the room. Alice and her boyfriend Austin seated next to each other. Both of them were white skin, blond hair and blue eyes, both from richer families. None of them looked worried, however. They are bothered, but it does not show.

A few seconds later...

Boom!

Detective Lamar and his officer friend Tate, looking highly esteemed step out into the waiting room full of brisk.

Detective Eric Lamar speaks with a highly elevated tone of voice, "Okay people, I know this has been a long day for you folks. We've been expecting one conclusion to be drawn."

Tate reads the test results aloud, "Austin Whitaker, you're free to go, Jorge Henandez, you can go too. Lance Weston, will you please join me and Detective Eric Lamar?"

The others leave with a whisk of sound a relief to go home and die now after the pressure it was for being there, being questioned about some dead school mate. Now it's Lance's turn to dive off a cliff for a minute or two.

"I'm afraid that leaves just you and me, son," said Eric.

"Wh-why me?" asked Lance.

"We've got a policy for you to follow. In my office, please," said Eric.

It was a minute and a half of debriefing the young boy, they made this loud and clear, and quick: "We just want to make sure that you did not kill Amanda Reyes and Ray Larson out of a fit of jealousy, psychopathy, or revenge, etcetera."

"Well I did not," said Lance.

Tate and Lamar asked Lance a dozen questions during their hearing.

And something else happens..... Somewhere out in the city an intruder strikes back at Will Wood High School.

That blonde haired reporter arrived just in the nick of time when she heard that a murderer had been wandering the campus at Will Wood High School.

She parked her car next to the curb, and made an extra precautious effort to avoid the police that blocked the front hall entry by simply taking a hike around the campus and enter from behind the back of the building. She reached the gym, and snuck right into the school library.

BOOM! She had made in without being stopped by the mercenaries.

The thick rich caramel scent of the school library filled her nostrils. She loved that smell. It felt like being in the presence of an important man. Like a city governor or something.

She took off her dark sunglasses and whipped out her camera and started taking publicity shots.

And then she made it. She found the scene of a heinous monster created by man out of electrician's holiday staff. A real work of art. A wall with pictures of Amanda Reyes, torn straight out of high school yearbooks, and blood paintings on the wall. It formed the words: HELL IS HOME! NOW PAY THE PRICE! REPAY ME NOW!

She snaps some shots of the horrifying display.

"What's this a knife?" Said Tabitha, the reporter.

She came to a saw blade jammed into the corner of a library desk made of wood. Lots of yearbooks stacked up on top.

"More to do with this Reyes girl," Tabitha shot another photograph.

A noise occurred, a squeaky rusty metal sound.

It came from that custodian's closet over there near the check-out stand.

Tabitha walked to the closet door, snapping a few more photos. And then she stops. She hears the squeaks again. She reaches down, grabs ahold the doorknob, pulls the door loose, and gave it a hard yank!

The door fell open, along with the body of a long dead janitor fell between the door frame and out the middle while hanging from his neck by a perfectly made noose. The dead janitor was pale, bald with long strands of hair around the sides of his head, a stab wound in his chest.

Tabitha screamed and dropped her bag of films.

A police officer walks into the school library, wondering what she was screaming about, and what had she found. "Miss, you gotta go!" Then he looks up at the dead man in the closet. "Son of a bitch!"

"Is this what you are looking for, officer?" Tabitha asked.

"Maybe. We were called in to inspect a bombing attempt. Broken windows. A burglary. But look at this shit!"

More happened that night…

Tabitha sorts through her photographs while ingesting the weekend of mayhem here in this hometown of Queen and Killer Kings.

She looks at the pictures of the dead janitor, then some more pictures of the Library. And then some…. Photographs of detective Lamar standing in front of Lance Weston's front yard, and a few more shots she took of him while visiting the crime scene where Amanda and Ray were killed.

Lance Weston sits at his bedside table, a dull low yellow lamp glowing in the barely lit bedroom, where he sits alone by the night, having a quiet moment in peace. His thoughts were a little rattled because of the nagging and complaining in today's lecture. His parents were mad. Being questioned by the two detectives sucked. And now he is feeling a post turbulent world of hate, fear, and sadness. An ex-girlfriend is dead, He tried to force down the hate he feels. He tried to be extra calm. He drank a mineral water to wash down the dull knot in his stomach. The numbness carried on through his mind, heart and feelings.

He nearly belched then and when a knock came at the door he continued to cry.

Another knock at the door followed by his dad's sounding call, "Lance?"

"Yeah? It's open."

His father entered the bedroom, "Are you doing okay?" He said.

Lance sighs, "Yeah, I'm fine. Do I look okay?"

"You look booked for a flight to London if you ask me."

"Well, yeah," Lance said, giving a brief sarcastic shrug of the shoulders. "There have been secrets involved, here, yeah. Can you get me something else? I'm beginning to dry these tears of mine."

"Is there a problem son?"

"Honestly? No!" Lance suggested. "There is NOT going to be any problems here."

"I know this is hard for you. I'm NOT going to let you shut yourself up in your room like this." His father said. He turns on the bedroom light.

The room lit up brightly.

Lance suddenly began to feel upbeat. The burning desire released from his flesh like a clear head of thoughts.

"Really?" Lance spazzes.

His dad grabbed a coat and bundled it around Lance's shoulders.

"You're coming to dinner with me and mom," said his dad.

"Okay, okay. I'm coming," Lance squeezes into his fine furs and off they go.

That night they went out for pizza.

Lance spent a nice evening together with his mom and dad and forgotten about the madness that occurred between his associate and his friend.

He pushed the disgusting memory of his unborn child and the mother that died with it, straight to the back of his mind.

His parents weren't as spunky about the sexually graphic details unlike most modern people may get.

Because mom and dad are secure and more normal now that most did when they got to be old as they were here now.

They had a discussion about how laws get when they occurred to fancy females like hers, and how they get when it's just as serious can be, when they have love. The threat of today, and a beginning of perfect people like us. And then let's go back and cut the cake, the cards, the oath, and the strict procedures of getting married. Now here's a toast. Quickly! Now one, two, three... POP! Are you next to pop a cavity? Like birthdate, and illness? Blood toasted oven mitts, and gloves. ----

----Now terror from within comes anew, a secret chore to be made.

One, two... Three!

Blood, blood, and blood in the future we all go! Now come see the truth!

You can't hide it anymore. THERE IS BLOOD OUT THERE READY TO COME BACK AND HAUNT YOU!

Sweet dreams, pal!

Lance sleeps soundly in his bedroom that night.

He dreams, and sees a grandfather clock, and hearing it ticking.

TICK! TOCK! TICK! TOCK! TICK!

He thinks that he is walking through the park and seeing a duck pond in the avenue. The place looks peaceful but that's only because no one is there, but something that cannot be seen, cannot be heard, but still may be noticeable is here. Some entity of some kind.

He gets the impression that life is moving on and he has got something to look forward to, except for now.....

.... He hears blood dripping from a knife.

No birds in the sky...

No wind blowing....

He hears whispering. It sounds like someone whispering the words, "Out of cold death, here we come!"

His nose starts bleeding. He drops to his knees and splashes his hands in the pond to rinse the blood away.

Amanda's corpse rises to the surface. And then it opens its pale faded eyes, and grabs him by the face.

The grandfather clock strikes 11:00 AM.

Lance sits up in bed.

It is raining outside.

Thunder that sounds like cannons firing bomb the sky away, the lightning flashes brighter than any bomb can do.

He looks outside his window and sees a silhouette of a dark person dressed in black, standing a block away from his house, staring at him.

Then the lightning flashes again a few more times just when the dark intruder appears then disappears.

Lance remembered lying awake at night constantly seeing who else did it and couldn't concentrate no more. And then he fell back asleep again and started dreaming some more.

There is something wrong with him.

CHAPTER 3

That same night Detective Eric Lamar seated at the kitchen table in his single bedroom apartment complex, rummaging through old notes and photographs he had snatched from older police files about the case of the missing stolen vehicle that belonged to Amanda Reyes.

He grabs the single frame black and white picture of the black luxury sedan that had the crack in the windshield.

He highlights the crack in the windshield with a black magic marker, and then scrubs off the license plate.

No one is going home tonight!

It's a deep dark blue day.

The funeral had just ended.

Lance stands before Amanda's grave, he kneels down to place a rose on top of the casket, when Eric suddenly approaches him from behind.

"Hello Lance!"

Lance nearly jumped out of his skin, "Detective, you scared me. What brings you here?" He straightened and smiles.

Eric forces a cracked smile, which is rare, "Just keeping an eye out on things... That's my job."

"True that," Lance said.

"I've been finding clues," Eric said, finally.

"Anything you know how to find?"

"I wish. Kid, I have a question for you. How many cars do you keep in your garage?" Eric instructed with a smile on behalf of the missing vehicle from Amanda Reyes point of being.

Lance opens the garage door, sunlight peeling the strength off of the engine block rested behind a town car, and a 1995 Hugger (Harley Davidson).

Eric began a lecturing, "A black Honda was stolen from Amanda's house on the night of her death, with a large crack in the windshield, and the license plates torn from the hinges." Eric spots the bike. "I like this," he grins facetiously.

"My brother's baby," Lance resigns.

"Does your brother race?"

"He once did. But not anymore. He passed away a few years ago," Lance twitches with nerve.

"I'm sorry," Eric said, with sympathy. He pauses and switches the objective, "It was my dream to race bikes like this when I was younger. But my father always wanted me to join the force. To be a patrol man. So that's what I became... An old family tradition."

"I hear you, now," Lance spoke.

"But you... You have a dream to follow, and you are walking right along with it, so to speak... Me? I should have walked away from my folks a long time ago. But instead my wife was the one who walked off. And so did my family... So now I am stuck in this town looking for other people, in clues that follow, not finding enough of my own, however. So now, the least you could do is make it easy for me and tell me what's causing all of this?" Eric Lamar demanded with full capacity of the general rules, which are, READ MY SOUL, AND GET BACK TO LIVING, NOW.

"You have me confused, Eric. Causing what?" Lance blurts off, with false occurrence in the mindfulness.

"The school library was broken into over the weekend. The yearbooks have been stolen with pictures of Amanda snipped out of them, then tacked to a bulleting clipboard on the wall. The man or girl who did this must have been obsession with Amanda. Pictures of her and her boyfriend were tacked onto the wall. And not only yours too. Do you read here what I am talking to you about now? Sorry. But no can do, now. But breathe deep. And sole witness to that event was yours truly. Man if I had the plan to make a necessary objection, I, would of course be the one to say, I have no stolen records in my portfolio, and yours kept on coming up with my case file work," Eric frowned. "Who could it be, Lance?"

Lance swallows hard, "I'm afraid I have no more clues here. But how many more times do I have to yell 'No, I did not, detective.'"

Down town, back in the police department, Eric and his partner Tate spend an afternoon till midnight discussing the murder case, in between snacking, reading, researching, and printing up lots of case working.

"It would have to have been a Saturday. And I think the school is closed for summer break," Eric said, with fast mean intellect.

"Negative… Summer classes started two weeks ago. However, not there. There have been a three day occurrence, and over the holiday. A third day in the offing," Tate answered.

"So where does that leave us?" Eric continued.

"How often do you mention this to anybody?" Tate asks.

"Just to Lance Weston," Eric sneered.

"And....?"

"Nothing."

"He's not a killer. Evidently Lance has never been to Amanda's house, either."

They stood there silently for a moment.

That night Eric had a dream that he was walking in the backyard of Amanda Reyes house, during the night of the crime. But this time, no one was there.

He discovers a coach bag on the ground.

He kneels down to unzip and finds it full of tools.

A shovel, a flashlight, and then----

----A blood drenched shoulder and a fist reach out, and it's Amanda's corpse emerging from the bag, screaming and roaring back to life, with a mouth full of blood and a decaying face filled with mud.

Eric wakes up from the dream to find himself laying still in bed.

It was just a nightmare...

The following day, a Thursday morning, Eric himself drives through a decent peaceful little suburban neighborhood of the upper class estates. Each side of the long twisting path is lined with bright beautiful pink three story houses.

He is on his way to pay a visit to a girl name Ashley, one of Amanda Reyes's cousins.

They kept this meeting confidential and it was short by the sequence. Eric interviewed Ashley while standing on the front porch, while being supervised by her younger brother Deran.

"How close were you to your cousin Amanda, Ashley?" Asks Eric.

"Amanda and I grew up together like sisters. I am younger than she was by two years," she scribed.

"What was she like?"

"She was fine," she frowned.

"Be a little more precise. Was she wicked? Was she fan of the opera?" Eric suggested.

"Umm... Well, she wasn't always the sweetest in the family. She got her way, always! It drove others bananas! But don't take this the wrong way, I loved her and everything, but going through a fresh line of boyfriends every semester was so not my thing. It didn't make the best for arguments sake. People defaced her in that sense," she teases.

"What can you tell me about her boyfriends?" Eric exclaimed a remark within a folding of a few brief mouth twisting, teeth baring grin. And a slight eyebrow twitch.

"They came and went so fast---," she laughs without mirth, "I don't know how to describe them."

Eric smiles, pauses frankly, and then waves a hand, gesturing to her to keep talking.

"Um, they were most likely the athletic types; football jocks, rich kids, I even seen her get into a car with a man who looked like he was in his mid-thirties," she said, almost glaring at her with psychic precision.

"Whoa. Wow. Okay..." Eric frowns.

"So...." Ashley said, declining the power of gesturing some more.

"A-hem! What do you know about a boy name Lance Weston?" Eric said.

"Lance? I'm not 100% sure about her involvement with Lance, but I kind of knew him personally," she definitely sights with him someplace.

Eric glanced down at his watch and exclaims it with, "Do you have a category with this man that I should know of?"

"No wait I remember... Some incident that happened with Lance, when one of Amanda's ex's found out that she was seeing him, there was a fight and Amanda broke up with Lance and got back together with her ex," Ashely grimaces intently, with satisfaction of the calmest gesture that be forgiven not to be. And then frowns some more again.

"Ouch! Over that? Was there a problem with Lance?" Eric was feeling like a talk show host sorting through the details of WHO BROKE UP WITH WHO? And WHO CHEATED? AND WHO IS THE REAL FATHER?

"He just wasn't willing to fight for her, I guess," Ashley smiles within a grimace and a frown.

"Oh. Okay. Who was her ex?" Eric asked, annoyed.

"Ray! That's his name. The boy that was murdered with her along with her," Ashley bounced on her heels, suddenly, empathically, and subjectedly.

Eric tenses up and lets out a long sigh...

Eric slouches in his seat behind his desk and nervously smokes a cigarette, and Tate sits in front of Eric's desk, reclining in his seat with both feet on the table.

Tate talks below the line while he chews a cigarette up and says, "Lamar, I know that you are quite fond of the boy. But frankly there are a few "curious" things about him."

Eric breathes a breath of air, "He got her pregnant and she left him for somebody else, that's it.

"I know. Right!" Tate gleamed between the teeth,

Eric slowed down the heart meter with a thumb tapping on the sheet of paper work on his desk in front of him, "Right, so there's more involvement between these two."

Tate sighs, glances at a few photos he had done. "Okay, pay the boy a visit."

"We cannot drop by after every story we hear. This one came from just one person," Eric exclaims with a slight push of the button on his desk. He yells, "Send Quentin to jail."

Tate squeezed lightly at the doorway frame while opening up a security deposit check first, "You have a job to do, Detective!"

"Right!"

"Bring him in, Eric." After a moments pause. "Do it now."

Lance was having fun with a girl next door when his cellphone rang and the message left was by Eric Lamar at the Forensic department at Theater Drive City Apartments complex.

He kissed her and tried terribly hard to squeeze away another ten minutes of touching and smiling and giggling with each other.

Then when ten came he had to go.

About this case: It's got to stop! Find the damn killer already.

Back at Eric's office, Lance shows up in agreement form, with Tate involved as a guest speaking into a microphone and recorder.

A tape rolling.

Q&A take two.

Lights, camera, Action!

We're rolling....

Eric gleams down at Lance, "We're going to ask you a few questions. And I know that we've been through of this before, but a few things have just come up."

"Go ahead, ask me more questions. How many times can I say that I'm not a killer? I'm innocent," Lance screamed.

Eric sighed softly, "I want you to tell us a story, Lance. And be very vivid with the details. We need you to."

Lance then sighed deeply, "Okay... Tell me where to begin."

Eric gleams with terror, "Tell us about your times with Amanda."

"The record button is on," Tate said, glancing at Lance.

"Begin," Eric said.

Eric and Tate look at Lance with a little bit of patience, then held their breath for a second, then paused, and exhaled, and then gleamed at him again.

"Do you not want to do this," asked Eric Lamar.

Lance looked up, "You want to know something?"

Eric and Tate listen intently.

Lance's face flushed, on the verge of tears, eyes burning with lust and forem, "I wanted it to end the moment it all began..."

The true story Lance had to tell took place in the evening, at a party at some drop in hotel apartment.

Lance was visiting, a party of 23 guests, rooms piled of people and classmates, so many that they all couldn't fit inside the apartment. There was a trail of beer drinkers leading in and out the front and back patio doors.

Lance was at this party, he had a few beers, the usual guests speaking, and there was danger somewhere here.

"It started for us at a party. Where I noticed her for the first time," said Lance.

The place was packed and it buzzed. The rooms including the bathrooms, hallways, and bedrooms with brightly lit with multicolored lighting gels, strobe lights, red, blue, green, and black light bulbs fixed in the electrical sockets.

Music blaring loud.

So far... The neighbors have not complained. They didn't seem to mind at times like this. We were brawling to the day.

Lance had a foul mouthed argument with his ex-girlfriend Brenda. She was mean and bitchy that night. She took Lance out the front door, and asks him, "What the hell are you doing here?"

"Nice to see you too, Brenda," Lance argues in agreement,

"A week after we break up, you show your face at my cousins birthday?" Brenda said, with grim reproach.

"You're cousin and I are okay. The fight is between you and me, not Sarah's. Look, why are you being like this? Let's go someplace else if you want to bitch!" Lance argued, suggestively.

"Right here is fine!" Brenda argues, regally.

Lance looked down, "Where is all of this coming from?"

"Your head on a stick, man!" Brenda yells,

"Fuck you, I've had it!" Lance said.

"Fuck you!" Brenda yelled.

Brenda slaps Lance with her purse. Her other boyfriend Lee squeezed between the two of them and pries them apart. Next he forcefully opens the match and puts both of them on the floor and then holds Brenda back from Lance.

Scott, one of Lance's close friends pushes aside the argument and stands in the middle between them and says, "Whoa! Stop this." He turns to Lance, "You okay man?"

"I'm fine," Lance agrees.

"Do you need anything?" asks Scott.

"I'm fine, I'm all done, man," Lance said, with a nod, a wink, and a smile.

"Okay. You need anything just let me know."

"Okay." Lance shrugs off the evening redness, fixes his shirt, collar, and smiles some more. He grabs a Hurricane, went out onto the back patio to fix up and have a booze, when suddenly Amanda came out of the dark and into the light and said," Slow down, hun. You'll throw it up again."

Lance almost pukes up his beer, "Jesus! Don't do that again!"

"Why date a woman so controlling anyway?" Amanda said.

"Who are you?" Lance answers with a nod.

Amanda shines in the glimmering light, with eyes of passion, seductive persuasion, and intimacy. "That girl was a bitch!"

"Ain't that the truth," Lance said.

"You fought her and that big man," Amanda says.

"So I did," Lance said.

"I really see no reason not to. You're cute you know?" Amanda grinned. She puts her hands on Lance.

"What are you supposed to do? Cook me spaghetti or something," Lance said, with a simple nod.

She looks at the room filled with head bangers and gasps, "Oh my god, it's my ex. Don't let him see me." She hides behind Lance like a squirrel crouching behind an elm tree.

"What's wrong with you?" Lance screamed.

"I can't let him know I'm down here," Amanda yelled.

"Well, he'll find you there eventually," Lance nodded.

Amanda bounced passed and said, "I've got an idea!" She snags his beer, "Put this down! Now let's go!" She bump rushes him into the party area and into the bathroom, lit by a red light bulb.

She slammed the door and locked it. "Just hold still," she said, with a sucking sound. She unzips his pants.

"What are you doing down there, girlie?" Lance smiles. And frowns.

"Just relax," she said, as she went down on her knees.

"Aw shit!" Lance groans as she gave him a blow job, in the bathroom, under the glare of the glimmering red light bulb on the ceiling, beside the fire alarm.

Lance grabs onto a towel rack and gave it a squeeze, grinds his teeth together, and takes the pain, the release, and the pleasure.

She comes back the next day.

It was a sunny day, Lance is working hard, digging up a manhole in the flower garden in the front lawn.

Amanda approaches the house, curiously, wearing a silky dress, and sandals.

"Hey boy," she asks.

Lance whirls around. Sweat dripping off his chin, on down to his muscular vibes, in his bare chest the muscles ached. "Hey," he said.

"Did I scare you?" Amanda asks.

"Not if I can help it."

"Look, let's get out! You and me."

"Will you be nice this time?" Lance asked away.

"Did I really do it?" Amanda asked again.

Lance swallowed hard and nodded.

"Don't worry, babe. I'll take care of you real good," Amanda said.

Lance and Amanda finish sex violently, and then they both fell asleep together and then the dream ends.

Alone again, Lance walks through Main Street, an old fashioned area, full of brick buildings, barber shops, delis, and antique shops here and there.

Something weird has begun.

Lance had been given some pretty bizarre looks from other people in town. And some of them were distant short term friends, and classmates.

Until one final step, he achieved fame for knocking up Amanda. He finds this irritably sharp, and coincidental by the time he had run into Scott, his local friend from school.

Lance addresses a heroic nod, "Hey man. What's gotten into you?"

"Lance, what's going on with you? Are you alright?" Scott gleams with sad approach.

"I'm fine," Lance nods twice.

"What the fuck did you do the other night?" Scott asks.

"What are you talking about?" Lance quivers for an offbeat chance at survival.

"That bitch you were with!"

"Brenda?"

"No! That girl Amanda. Tell me you didn't sleep with her," Scott grimaces, with a cold look in his eye.

Lance grins. "What's this about anyway?"

"That girl is a bitch, she makes Brenda look like a saint, in comparison."

"Do we need to discuss this here?" Lance asked, enthused with proposal.

"I tried phone calling you and you did not answer," Scott proclaimed.

Lance reached for his mobile device to see that his cellphone is missing. "Damn!"

"Oh well, anyways, if you have got something to answer for this jock guy is out for justice. She got back with her old boyfriend and I hear he is itching to find you. So hurry up. Grab a moto scooter and ride up on out of here," Scott proclaims, standing still.

"Shit!"

"If anything happens, remember to call me first, alright?" Scott suggested, with a hand waving in front of his face, meaning keep it down low.

"Later," Lance said.

When Lance returned home, he made a call to Amanda and then a man answered the phone. He sounded like he was asleep. Awoken by the phone ringing and Lance did not bother to say anything, and he gently hanged up the phone.

Back at the station, Lance tells Tate and Lamar the finishing end to his story.

"As the days went by I started receiving threatening letters. One of them being a cryptic note with clipped up newspaper, and magazine headlines, pasted onto a plaster board saying, "LET HER GO!"

And the tape recorder is stopped with sudden brief inquiry, a news broadcast is now in session.

Tate book ended the matter briefly, "Eric, let me have a word with you."

Eric and Tate left the board meeting and stepped outside, and they both lit a few cigarettes and continued a background moment.

"So, what do you think?" Eric asked.

"They are not too sure if he comes down here to solve the case here, there are muddles of film and right to act to be on camera for the pictures we granted here by letting him stay here the night, let's go," Tate grimaced.

"He told the truth, let's have a moment here," Eric suggested.

And they went back in the meeting room and allowed Lance to call home, grab his things, and come to visit Lance at a hotel for gathering suspects later. Keep him off the streets, keep him here, and keep him safe until Chicago comes.

Tate added, "Others say she knew Ray for a couple of days, when Lance says they knew each other longer."

"But that also matches Ashley's story," Eric said.

"Ashley?" Tate asked.

"Amanda's cousin, I interviewed her," Eric sighs, "So, that's it."

"Eric, I have a suggestion to make, keep him profile while I do some back up work. Just a few. Hold on," Tate briefly discovered a new victim of the case. He enthusiastically exchanged object upon opinion matters elsewhere and then BOOM!

Eric came back to Lance and said, "Your story was a lot of help. Just out of curiosity, how did you know about the cryptic letter?"

"I received one," Lance said.

Tate breaks in briefly, "Do you know about the one the police received during the night of the murders?"

"No..." Lance said.

"Where is the one you received?" Tate observantly quoted.

"I threw it away," Lance said.

Silence.

"I want to hold you overnight while we examine the evidence again," Tate said.

"You're not putting me behind bars!" Lance erupts.

Eric eases him, "It's not jail. You'll be here, in this building, just for tonight..."

Tate suggested that Lance relaxes and that they are taking care of him.

Eric leaves the police station, walks out to his car which was parked across the street, and as he crosses it, meanwhile reaching into his coat pockets for the keys and suddenly gets hit by a speeding Buick. Its license plate is missing. It just so happens to be Amanda Reyes missing car.

The driver, apparently who stole this car, back tracked a few steps and, then drove to him with the headlights off, silent and, quickly. But when it hit, Eric took a leap, and a tumble so carefully and gleefully it saved his life.

The car nearly hit him first!

It was about ten inches back when he jumped, almost a hop, and turned sideways and rolled on his way up and down the windshield. He finished his tumble and whirled around as he made it over the windshield, and then off he went with a clever bounce down to the trunk and plopped onto the cement.

As he lay there in the middle of the road, motionless and seemingly afraid that it was close and he then lay down and slept for a minute in the street.

He landed pretty hard on his hands and knees. Then he turned over on his back and slept the night away for what seemed like days...

But a minute later he was woken by his partner Tate.

"Eric! Lamar! Wake up!" Screamed Tate.

Eric lays on the ground with a trickle of blood out of the corner of his mouth. He had bit his cheek. His eyes flickered open.

"Get up boy, you're in the street!" Tate lifts Detective Eric Lamar and pulls him up and carefully shifts him right side up, and then takes him over to the sidewalk. "Just relax."

They sit to catch their breath.

Eric moans deeply.

And Tate pulls out a cigarette, Eric accepts it, and Tate offers a light to him.

A doctor on staff treated Eric's wounds. Luckily he moved with persistence and survived without a broken bone in his body. Just a few scrapes on his hands and knees. And his back was a little sore. But nothing too bad.

Eric told his supervisor that he had managed to safely regard the vehicle. And it was the same car that was stolen from Amanda Reyes house during the day it occurred.

The murderer stole the vehicle and tried to end his life today.

But first, Eric needs to go back to his private sectors and sleep it off.

Before the night was over, Tate made remarks about Eric's surviving the hit and run attempt, calling him, "The man made of steel." And, "Eric the acrobat!"

Surprisingly Eric managed to laugh a few good times.

Now Eric needs to get home and sleep well for a night or two.

But before he left, he told Tate and his boss Richter about the car that hit him, and he recognized the car (Amanda's stolen Buick), but he could not see the driver behind the wheel.

They agreed on a few things: The act of running a man over sounded niggard; the act of a homicidal woman, or a jealous lover. And it seemed almost like a demented child molester the fact that the killer could not hit the brakes in time before he went jealous. It was gay how he decided to continue his killings here.

Another thing, the license plate was missing, unmarked vehicle. Another cut-and-paste cryptic style letter was found on the ground outside on the street which read: LEAVE ME ALONE NOW!

They know the killer is someone else. So they let Lance Weston go for now.

CHAPTER 4

Tabitha, the blond haired news reporter, had taken her reels of film to the lab and had them transferred to 8x10's and closely examined them.

She took a few photos of Lamar bringing Lance in, and a few shots of Tate bringing Lamar to the curb of the road, it was the night the killer had tried to kill Lamar with the stolen vehicle.

She saw the driver.

Someone familiar too.

"Oh my God!" Tabitha said, as she grabbed her cellphone to make a call. Then…

The lights in the workshop went off with a sound of a SNAP! It was the circuit breaker.

To her horror everything went new again. Nobody has this place. Nobody….

Tabitha lowered herself at ground level and crouched beneath a table.

Whoever done this is standing outside. Nearby. Or someplace...

So, Tabitha decided to wait here until help arrives. She dialed for the police on her cell phone.

A flickering light went off, with a scent of gravy, like gasoline. The flame throwing was visible from her end somewhere from the hallway.

She knew right then, the suspect who cut the circuit breaker had lit a fuse, now there is no escape. Unless Tabby can survive a twelve feet drop from the shutter doors.

At this moment, Tabitha was sensitive, she could now imagine getting off with better facial hair. In her mind she realized how much she now appreciates life. Like often times, she would curse at the alarm clock, and being ungrateful at times. But waking up at 5:30 A.M. is better than not waking up at all. Locking herself out of her apartment without a spare key is better than burning alive.

She crawled on her hands and knees to escape the toxic smelling fumes. She reached the side wall and climbed up on top of the garbage dispensers and stood up high on a stack of boxes. She propped open a window, crawled away really fast and took a dive from the window, and landed hard on an open dumpster.

She climbs away and stands upright on the lid, and lifts off to safety.

Now, she appreciates being alive!

She now calls in the emergency, asks for the Police, the Fire Patrol, and the Paramedics.

All of her furniture is gone, her secret film lab is destroyed, and all of the evidence is now hashed up.

But now who is it that started the fire? Who did this???

"Damn you!" she said.

The Fire Department soon to rescue, while they continued to put out the fire Tabitha has a moment to talk with Tate.

She says, her evidence has been laid to rest, in regards to this unfortunate accident. She also explained that the circuit breaker had been cut off, she didn't see who did the blackout but has a good idea that it was the suspect who had been driving the stolen Buick of Lance's case.

Tate needed this chat for the records and put a search warrant out for the missing recovery.

She also stated that the stolen Buick had been sighted near an old house out in the hills where three youths were killed during a graduation party for Seniors of Will Wood High.

She tied a few strands for the report and Tate argued that it was completely misforgiveness; that there is no cover for the Lance Weston trial, if not beaten into him enough. "I made a mistake," he said, "I will continue the Weston recovery and thoroughly instigate a cover charge for the missing Buick crime. P.S. I don't care where or when, but I do find it unforgiveable enough to shut down Will Wood High without proposal. Peace.

Tabitha said one more thing, "The driver of the stolen Buick who looks just like Amanda, tried to kill again. It was her who drove it through the street that night that nearly killed me tonight, and Lamar yesterday.

The early sun rose quickly and began to light the sky at 6:00 A.M. A low cast of sun took the beams away and now the fire is gone.

Inside the warehouse where Tabitha's photos were placed, the vandal arsonist duct taped a new message on the wall. A big one! It read: GET OFF THIS PLACE OR DIE!

"We got another one," said the Sherriff.

What next? Tabitha cringed at the moment of thought.

Eric Lamar lay tossing and turning in bed, having a bad dream.

He saw the outside of a house. Amanda standing outside like a cadaver on wheels. She plowed through the place like hover lifting. He saw Lance who stood near while complaining about a short distance nearness. He looked away down the street he saw an ocean.

He hears a voice screaming the words: "Detective! You are annoying!"

According to this variation of the dream is that it takes place before he joined the force, and here he is talking to his suspects. According to his knowledge if that were the case, his dream slowly derivitates the fact that ancient knowing of Detective Tate's skin is dead. His throat had gone missing...

In his head, during this dream, his detective mate is known to be dead. He gasps when Tate suddenly steps up from behind him with his throat slit, and eyes wide like disaster.

Eric gasps, at the sound of the phone ringing. He's awake now.

He answered the phone. It is Tate informing him about a meeting due to lab crisis. He will be here soon to inform him about a recent event.

Later that night, Eric heard a rapping at the door. He answered it and found Tabitha at the door.

"Hello Eric Lamar, I'm Tabatha Sommerset, I'm with the Chronicle Review Report, may I have a moment of your time?"

"Sure, come on in," Eric allowed her in with a sigh.

They sat together at the table.

"You were the one who was found at the site at one of the warehouses on Vermont Street that burned?"

"Yes, I spoke with your partner, and then I asked him if I can speak with you about this case about the Reyes kid."

"I can leave without a lie. My detective friend may seem kind of like a halfwit at times, but I don't do cover interviews to short time prophets like you," Eric said, with boring honesty.

"Well, I trust you because you're a little less moralist about the case than he was. But since my photos and cover stories of the recent months have been destroyed due to a vandalist who torched my lab by setting it afire, I hoped there could be something I can give you to help nail this son of a bitch," Tabitha swore.

"Is there anything I can do to persuade you none of this will record on paper since I am this bastard friend of mine sidekick?" Eric gasped at her.

"There's more to the case than an elaborate drunk. I have received her photographs since last year, back east somewhere there was a kid who offed her own existence because of a letter that she received told her that she is a twin," Tabitha announced. "Low has it been for her since. And the Amanda girl, who was murdered last week, ain't been told. And her rage was not the beginning. The first hacked were three kids, one boy and two girls were sliced and diced during graduation night, somewhere in a house up in the hills. Three Will Wood High students."

"This girl did it. The same one that killed Amanda and Ray?"

"Death is only the beginning. She is not her type no more. She's supernatural. She is a devil. She is eternal. And she's killing again," Tabitha smarted.

The hand written page about the three graduates that were murdered out in the woods, written down by Tabitha Sommerset, quickly read on by Eric Lamar.

THREE DEAD, AT GRADUATION NIGHT PARTY!

Fifteen high school kids throw a party on a Lake Shore Blvd. house in the woods. It is Graduation Night.

Marcy Wright and Billy G. share a picnic out by the yard. They both have been drinking that night. And the two decided to smoke out back.

"An intruder from out in the forest stabbed Billy in the chest," says O'Ryan, a party goer, who witnessed a killing from the upstairs bedroom window. He said, the killer quickly marched up to Marcy and Billy Gomes and stabbed Billy in the shoulder, and then deep into the chest. Marcy let out a shrill cry. She ran. But before long she was struck dead when the killer (dressed in dark black; almost like a ninja) threw the dagger from across the yard and hit straight in the back. The blade wedged deep in the center of her back. Marcy fell and went beyond dead.

Everyone there went straight for a park and ludicrously vanished between the place. And somewhere in the park road we found a girl name Melissa Aimes, struck down by a speeding truck.

Six of us called the police on our phones.

Our cars were clipped. None of them would start.

Adamson who had went out to grab us smokes and booze was on his way back from the store. We car pooled in his truck.

And later they were questioned by the police.

Eric went through it, reading the pamphlet for the first time. Argued why he needed a clue like this.

That night he and Tabitha spent a warm and cool night underneath the bed covers.

That night, Eric had yet another dream.

He saw Lance standing over the edge of a cliffside with a grave marker that had his first and last name printed on it.

Lance said, "I AM DEAD NOW!"

Eric looked all around himself, and saw that he was surrounded in many graves. Then screams from underground broke out in one loud screams. The dead bodied in their graves began screaming like an angry crowd bursting with cheers from under ground. The earth beneath him began to shake. It felt like it would soon give away from beneath.

He wakes up with a slight jolt.

Later that evening, Tabitha got dressed and applied her makeup and laundry to her body. And Eric gave himself a close examining at the mirror door. Then he said, "My scars, and bruises have been healing. And so is my heart."

"How are your legs?" Tabitha smartened.

"I'll never tell," said Eric.

She needed to go to her collections office and claim her fortune to repay the Sheriff for gathering her funds to build a new deck. Her lab will practically be rebuilt.

She kissed Eric goodnight and left for a moment.

Eric sat there feeling fibbed. He had just got done sleeping with an error of his new ways.

CHAPTER

5

Late in the new day, Tate went for a drive across the valley. He has been called in to take a tour through a house where a recent murder had occurred.

As he drove to this far off county location of Greensburg, he replayed a few moments of conduct with Eric.

The day that Eric questioned Lance for the first time, Tate had driven Lance's house, but he did not stay. He went into town instead. He was being followed by a Buick that was missing the front plate and the person driving it looked a lot like Amanda.

He asked Eric if he has ever felt like a stranger among him. And Eric told him that he did all the time. And the pressure of his job felt like a stranger. And it's the type you never get used to.

Tate told him that it was well worth mentioning because he never felt love for him the way he did today, Eric told him to relay the past somewhere dignified, and he coarsely screwed himself!

Tate frowned at him and laughed himself silly! Tonight may be the best part reality could bring. Tonight is the best part reality will bring.

Because Cincinnati won!

They grimaced at one another and fabled to speak again until this curfew has been sanctioned by the police captain.

Today though however Tate had been followed in his car all the way over to Grassboro, a company neighborhood park in Greensburg. He was informed that a Natalie Walker has been sighted over a month and a half ago, and now her parents are missing. He parked his car in front of the two story house, and the person following him peeled off to the curb and stopped someplace around the field.

Tate came up to the front porch to find the front door jammed shut. It looks demolished, like a man with a three gun sedan just crashed right through it. Somewhere in the report it said, the knob to the front door is missing. Second of all the electricity had been shut off. No dogs in the backyard. Bring a flashlight.

Tate jogged around the yard, climbed an explicitly loaded backyard fence, and climbed right through the garage entrance. The doorway was unevenly caved in, like something big strong and heavy crumbled the side roof with a three ton stomp, bang, thrust, and crush.

It smelled musty, dusty, and rank. It made Tate dry cough in his handkerchief.

Tate took a brief tour while having looked through the windows, he aimed his flashlight bulb in the dankest pursuits everywhere and watched them slowly wither to pieces after death. The knob holes in the garage were filled with apache water slides. It had been caved in from the top.

Tate nodded, they said abandoned for a month and a half, these houses were built five years ago, and this place is looking like a ruined ancient scrap heap. Like one of those cabins you would find in a ghost town near Collinsville.

Something felt a bit strange, like a lurker from the depths of the Amityville basement reaching up and crawling into his mind, telling him to GET OUT!

He reached for his phone, then whirled around intensely, and drawed out his pistol.

Nothing escaped!

He called up the police and asked to have a few more days to quickly wrap up gear and explore the house. Whoever smashed the roof, and busted off the front door had left no solitary example to conclude the chase. This is party city!

Tate closed the receiver and shouted, "Whoaaa baby!" And he jogged back to the front of the house and slid behind the wheel, turned on the Mexican music station and be bopped on his way to the cabin where the three high school graduates were murdered.

Late in that evening, Eric Lamar hopped across the room near a kitchen stand and plopped on a seat at the kitchen table. He was about to eat some rice and salad when he received a disturbing complaint via phone message. And when he had he wished he had been certain about the Amanda case.

He was told that Amanda's casket was removed from the earth for some basic testing research and found it to be empty, Her corpse therefore was removed from the lab during an autopsy and missing ever since then.

He sat quiet.

Nobody on this earth needs to breed with each other no more. This is falluting bullshit, he said under his teeth.

He told them he would need to get in touch with Tate and warn him of hidden clues to be searched from. This had not yet begun to hit the fan yet,

He switched places for the evening and ran a cold bath. His sick leave must end prematurely.

Meanwhile, elsewhere, Tabitha had broken into some secret files and gasped with shocking experience when she had discovered who had who when and how removed from the deck.

She knows now.

Amanda's pregnant belly was stabbed late one night. But now it's a different case. Because of all things now that she had been murdered. But the case is now evidentially proven to exist for the matter, her child survived.

Tate rounded up tapes of the investigation and found that a nearby sewer system had been broken through. Something else was the matter and it had Dodge City written all over it. The facts in the case serve rivalry and justice for a better answer. Everybody corned awake and served them breakfast for a different day. More teenagers will be sliced and gone today and, tomorrow morning.

He parked his car in front of the old house behind the hills where three were butchered during graduation day.

Tate casually walked through, the front door open, the locks have been busted for the matter. He walked right on through.

And he took a brief tour through the place and now it appeared to be unofficial since now it appeared to be dead rotten through the bridges over Madison County. The house had been blown to bits.

He walked through the living room area, found the stairs, and toured through the bedrooms, checked the stinking bathrooms, and marched back down the stairs.

The sun had gone down, the moon is full, and everything was well lit dark blue now. He worked his pressure up brought a flashlight to see better in the darkened corners of the entire place.

He heard a scratching sound, and then a growl, a snapping sound, and then a bark and a growl.

He whipped up his revolver and aimed it around the surrounding places.

Something vicious clambered through the raided home front and leaped up and took a bite through Tate's arm, releasing his strap and ripped his arm open. And Tate through himself out the back door. It was a sliding glass door. And the glass was crushed and Tate landed on the back porch.

The thing that bit him was a coyote and it made a fierce snap at his feet.

Tate quickly snapped the revolver back in place, aimed it high at the ceiling, fired off a round, hitting the chandelier, it broke, and fell on the coyote, in paling it through the neck.

The dog yelped!

It died!

And then suddenly another one leaped out of the dark and landed on his face. Before it could bite his tongue out through his nostril Tate stuck the barrel end of his gun in its neck, then pulled the trigger, piercing it's snout, and a glob of blood splashed out through the top of its head along with the coyotes brain.

Tate screamed, "God darn it!"

Where the hell did these two get from? He imagined it was possible to land a job like this elsewhere. With a little bit of practice he could solve the crime hit and miss wise. They act like there are no witnesses. There are.

The dead have risen from the graves.

There will be no more next time around.

Tate measured up with defeat when his head exploded.

The killer defeated Tate with a grenade by firing his old pistol into his skull. And then there was no room left to kill but yourself.

The killer dressed in dark clothing motioned through the dark and began collecting wolf's brains.

The killer kind of cleaned the place up by having the gun cleaned off and removed privately.

Tate's cellphone began to ring. It was Eric. He leaves a message that will not be returned or heard.

Eric said into the microphone, "Hey Tate, listen up, we got to get together, as of now. I just got a phone call from the station. They said that Amanda's body was stolen. They discovered this last night. Her casket has been removed and found it empty. It's 7:45 P.M. on my clock. I'll see you at the office in fifteen. See you then." And then the voice mail message center left a beep saying: YOU HAVE 1 NEW UNHEARD VOICE MESSAGE.

Parked outside was Amanda's Buick. And somewhere inside the house was her stolen body.

The killer sat quiet and analyzed the cop's blood.

In the killers threat, blood will follow its way again.

The killer got back into Amanda's vehicle and drove away and headed for town.

Somewhere in town Tabitha tried to reach out to Eric, and Eric was at home and about ready to leave to join his cronies at work.

CHAPTER 6

Lance is awake now, he had been resting in a hidden room at the station, and the moment he saw Eric limping his way into the room and told him that he is free to go home now.

"Thanks," Lance said.

"Don't mention it," Eric said.

"Do you want to tell me what this is for?" Lance asked.

"Let's just say you are free to go, now move," Eric said, as he stepped out of the office, limping on his left leg, steady gripping fast on his walking stick.

"Wait, you lock me up for a night and you can't tell me what happened?" Lance suggested him to answer.

"It's not my job," Eric said.

"Talk to me damn it!"

"Listen, you just go home Lance. Just be happy that you are safe."

Lance right now doesn't know yet about Amanda's body missing from the lab, and it's grave,

"Am I next?" Lance demanded a new response.

"Just go home, and I'll drop by afterwards," Eric walks away.

They both go outside and the killer is across the street watching them two argue.

It's a crisp cool night, nobody on the streets, except for Lance, Eric, and the killer.

"If I'm not next, somebody else is!" Lance cried out in shame.

Lance turns around and runs down the street from an opposite view point.

Somewhere else, Jorge Hernandez sleeps on the couch at home, the lights are off. It is quiet and peaceful.

The phone rings.

He wakes up moping and groaning when he answers it.

"Yeah?" He said into the phone. "Casey?",---- "Nah, nothing. I was asleep.,------You need me to come get you?,---- "I'll be home.", ------ "Later." And he hangs up the phone.

Jorge tries to go back to sleep. And then the doorbell rings, suddenly.

Jorge climbs up to his feet and walks slowly down to the front door, kicks the coffee table by accident, "Shit!" he cried. He limps his way to the front door and opens it. Nobody there. He slams the door, turns around and heads for the living room and when suddenly the looter knocks on the door this time. Irritated, he reaches down and grabs a crowbar from the utility case, propped near the closet outside the front entry.

The weapon hangs at his sides, he lifts it up, ready to swing it down if the man at the door so happens to be an intruder. He reaches for the doorknob with his free hand, and suddenly doorbell rings rapidly a bunch of times, causing him to lapse in thought and drop the weapon.

Jorge takes a deep breath and opens the door to find it vacant, then he charges outside ready to fight!

He charges down the front porch ready to hurrah, then stops again when he finds his Ford Navigator vandalized.

The hood of his truck is open, the car battery removed from its engine.

"What the fuck?" Jorge growled. He walked a few steps near and finds his spark plugs snipped away, the hoses and his radiator busted through. "Son of a bitch!" He whines.

He turns around and sees a silhouette of the intruder standing at the front door.

"Hey!" Jorge yelled, and he ran for the killer, ready to brawl, fight, and club him with his crowbar.

The stranger slams the door. Something electrical propped up on the doorknob. His car battery. The front porch wet with mud and water. When Jorge reached down and grabbed for the doorknob he was electrocuted. His hand burned off. His head exploded.

Sparks are flying. His body burned. Executed all over the place.

At the mortuary Eric Lamar paid a visit to search some questions about what had caused Amanda's corpse to up and leave during the autopsy.

"It was the most ridiculous incident I've ever seen," Myron Madsen, the mortuary attendant repeated, "The mortician had been embalmed just like one of the corpses would have been."

Eric stood with quality while he watched some of the surveillance footage taken during the riot act in the mortician's room.

In the autopsy filmed, Benson Glare remedied the tools as necessary, then somebody dressed all up in black, with a face covered in dark nylon steps into the room, grabs Benson by the throat and stabs him with the embalming needle. He screams in agony and vomits a viscous fluid.

Then the killer drops the knife into his skin tight overalls and leaves. An hour later the killer vanishes. And then suddenly Amanda's body steps right out from the curtain and gently leaves while wearing nothing but a curtain over her half naked corpse.

"Oh shit!" Eric gasps.

"What is it? Is something wrong?" Myron asked.

Eric suddenly began to get brain puzzled.

"After the police investigated the crime scene I found this on the front steps out in front of the queen complex," Myron holds forth a cryptic note.

The letter is blood stained, conceived with letters cut out of headlines from magazines and newspaper articles. It said: SHE IS MINE... 442 CABIN, LAKEWOOD.

It's the address to the old house behind the hills where their graduation night party had taken place.

Lance discovered the messy killing of Jorge. A racked up corpse has been sighted on the front porch. "Oh god." He said. Lance leaves on foot.

Tabitha returns to her warehouse, the one that had been practically destroyed by the fire that happened last week. She propped shutter windows open to let in the air, while she dishes out some security locked boxes she kept full of emergency money, and back up files with all of her saved photographs on them.

She put a wad of cash in her purse, then withdrawled a few security photographs. A picture of Lance leaving the office during the time he was taken into Lamar's office for questions and answers.

The lights in her warehouse suddenly grew dim.

She looks up and gasps in shock. And she coughs when she breaths in a rancid dead fish smell.

The sound of footsteps, and heavy breathing echoes through out the halls of her secret workstation.

The smell became unbearable.

The loud breathing echoes sounded like a dinosaur roaring in reverse.

"I gotta get out of here," Tabitha smarted, while gathering up her clues and left the place behind.

The slow paced footstep sounds began to be more rapid, almost in a running step motion, and they sounded like they were catching up to her.

Tabitha screamed and fled the building and jumped inside her car. She started the engine and fled the scene.

She drove away and dialed Lamar on her cellphone.

Casey, young, latina, and she's Jorge's girlfriend stands out front of a crossways diner. She exits the front of the building to get in her Suburban when she is suddenly crossed by Lance.

"Casey!"

"Aren't you supposed to be locked up?" Casey scowls.

"Don't go home Casey, you're in danger!" Lance screams.

"No! I don't need any stress or your bullshit, Lance."

Lance grabs her by the arm and says, "Listen to me, you don't want to go back! Come with me to the police station!"

Casey jerks her arm back out of his grip, "You're crazy! We're not a part of your drama, anymore."

She gets inside her truck.

Lance pounds a fist on the hood and yells, "Stupid bitch! You better listen to me, your boyfriend is dead. They murdered him, his body is on the front porch of his house, he's dead, DEAD, he's FUCKING DEAD!"

Casey's eyes were wet with tears, her face is full of fear. "Just get away from me, you freak!" She starts the engine, puts the car in reverse, and drives away.

"No!" Lance hollered. "Damn it!"

While she drives away, Casey dials Jorge's number and puts it through to the speakers. The dial tone beeps loudly as she drives.

"Jorge, come on baby, please answer," she said, crying her eyes out.

The dial tone stops and she hears the recorded message, THE SUBSCRIBER YOU CALLED DOES NOT ANSWER, PLEASE LEAVE A MESSAGE AFTER THE BEEP!

"Shit!" She scowled, angrily.

She pulls over and stops before a red light glare, she turns on the dome light and finds a yearbook picture of her and Amanda tacked onto the horn of her steering wheel and said, "What the hell is this?"

Two hands, wearing tight black gloves rise up behind her face, and wrap a coil of brass copper wire around Casey's throat, and strangle her. She chokes as she scratches at the wire. She bleeds out through the corners of her mouth. And her eyes are open with shock! And surprise....

Her foot steps down on the gas pedal and the car swerves down the road, while jerking from left to ride, stop, and then go, then stop and go again!

Her throat splits open, and the suburban comes to a slow finish.

The killer steps out of the car and walks step by step away as the car suddenly dies and then blows up.

Fire was everywhere!

And in the mean time they're staying there.... DEAD!

CHAPTER 7

Lance dials Eric Lamar on his cellphone and he answers, "This is Eric."

"Eric! Listen to me, there's been trouble! Jorge Hernandez has been murdered!" Lance said.

"What? Lance you were supposed to go home. Why didn't you?" Eric hissed.

"It's still happening!"

"Are you sure he's dead?" Eric asked.

"I'm positive. Just take a look at the mess out front."

"Another note was discovered, this time it was at the mortuary. It said LAKEWOOD."

"Lakewood?" Lance asked.

"You know where it is?" Eric calmed down a bit.

"Lakewood is a resort where we all had our graduation party. Amanda was there too. That's where we had the big conflict, with her boyfriend. Cabin 442 Lakewood, right?" Lance added up and asked.

Eric just remembered that Tate was heading off to the house on Lakewood. The cabin behind the hills where the three murder victims partied. "Shit," he whispered.

"The other suspects are going to die tonight, but I don't know where they live." Lance said with a sigh.

"Where are you at?" Eric asked.

"I can't answer that, I'm going to Lakewood!" Lance screamed.

"Stay where you are!"

Lance hanged up.

In a nice suburban valley home nearby Austin and Alecia spend a quiet evening at home together. They were two suspects that had previously seen Amanda a day or so before her death. And now they live on and go about the daily routine. Life without a doubt.

"Austin, I'm coming out, would you close the window blinds, please?" Alicia said.

"Sure, of course," Austin said, reaching up to the window and pulling down the shades.

Somebody is outside. They are being watched.

"Are they closed yet?" Alicia hollered from the shower.

"Yes they are, baby," Austin added some more.

"Good," she said, stepping out from the bathroom naked while drying her wet blond hair with a cleaning towel. "How do I look?"

"Gorgeous," Austin said.

"Come and do my back," Alicia smiled, holding out a bottle of oil to him.

"Whatever you say," Austin gladly did so with a smile.

On a city street, secluded in night time observation, Lance jogs down the street alone. When suddenly, a police car stops him with the searchlight and the sound of a horn with the police lights already shining on him.

"Hey son! You mind stopping for a bit?" Said the officer.

"Why officer, for speeding?" Lance said, catching a few breaths.

"You look like you're in a hurry, what's the problem?"

"The way I see it, I'm not moving fast enough," Lance grimaced, with a shrug of the shoulders.

The officer gets out of the car and aims a flashlight at him.

"Where are going at this hour?"

"Need to see a friend, officer," Lance said, almost sorry now.

"Hop in, I'll take you there," said the officer.

"I have do it alone, sorry," said Lance.

"I can still take you. Don't worry," said the cop.

"I don't think you understand," Lance coughed.

The cop received a message from a fellow officer, and then he turns progressive with a shrug and a tight gesture, "Hold it. Are you Lance Weston?"

Lance sighs with a "Grrr!"

Austin and Alicia have sex and afterwards they finish the top of night with salad and beer while they have a discussion and about Gabby and Rob's birthday party next week. They talk diligently for a half an hour before they heard the alarming sound of a window breaking somewhere downstairs.

"What was that?" Alicia asked.

"Sounds like it came from out back," Austin said, taking a sip of beer.

"Out back?" Alicia yells.

"The backyard! Hold on, I'll go check," Austin said, putting his beer down and getting up out of bed.

He put a shirt on, pajama pants, and sneakers and went downstairs.

Alicia was baffled. She put a robe on tight and fixed her hair up in a little bun.

Downstairs, Austin leaped out into the backyard while hollering, "Is someone there?"

He found the back door of the garage open, the window was broken.

"Is somebody there?" He added.

Whoever it is, he or she is not responding.

Austin slowly walked through the open door, and turned on the light.

Broken glass was everywhere.

When suddenly a fire poker was thrust into his spine and it stabbed through his chest, blood spewing out of his mouth, vital fluids sprang from his chest and he was dead! The killer dressed in black, with the black nylon over the face stood there and stared down at Austin's dirty corpse.

Inside, Alicia came down the stairs to put a pot of hot water on the stove to have some tea.

"Austin, are you alright out there?" Alicia vibed. She looks down at the kitchen sink, "Austin, honey, when I ask you to do the dishes, that doesn't mean wait until I'm the one to do them next." A pause. Silent. And then she said, "You hear me?" With a weak cry,

She peered through the kitchen window, her vision blurred, then focused in to see Austin laying down in the backyard with blood on his mouth, throat, and chest.

She gasped.

The killer grabs her hair from behind, slams the stove top, throwing out the pot of hot water, and

presses her face down on the hot irons, making Alicia scream in pain, her face burned into a crisp, and then she died.

The killer dropped her to the floor and left the house alone.

CHAPTER 8

The police car pulls up to Austin and Alicia's house.

"Is this it?" Asked the officer in charge.

"I'm positive but I think we're already too late," Lance moaned and groaned.

In spite of what he just said the officer drew his pistol and walked up to the front step. He held his gun tight, reached in and grabbed the radio and called into headquarters, "I'm at 457 Where Wood Lane, the house looks broken into."

A piece of paper floating in the breeze brushes against Lance's window seat. He grabs it and reads it, and it said: COME TO THE CABIN.... I AM WAITING, LOVER!

Lance sneaks away from the patrol car.

The officer on deck says, "Boss, he's there and here saying he's been expecting a riot somewhere.

A boy name Lance Weston---" The officer turns around to find that Lance had gotten away. And he said, "---What the hell is happening here?"

Eric rides passenger side with a fellow officer name Richter who navigates him on the way to this peaceful cabin on Lakewood.

It's a chilly late night evening, the ride to the cabin was smooth, the car he drove in was safe, secure, and sound.

"Lakewood is a sleepy time town museum of faithful rows of steep cliffs, anarchy punks, and houses. It's mostly private types out in the boondocks. The sticks. Night owls like to park to get drunk and piss on the riverside."

"According to Lance's story, that is where the graduation took place."

"Is he here?" Richter asked.

"I'm afraid so."

"Shoot, darn it. He ought to be at home."

"He's superintendent of the Lakewood people. He almost drawn to it."

"What a melodramatic apeshit, you're too good to these people. Wisen up, Eric, would you." Richter suggested.

Eric smiled with the corner of his eyes.

Lance had sprinted through these backroads to the house on Lakewood, and he made it all the way there.

He stood open to it. Gazing up at its dark two story features, and the attic perched on top of its secondary hole thrusters!

He died a moment too soon, he suggested.

The lights were dead out!

He needed no courage the slightest upon entering. He seemed to feel elegant to it's two story features. Hyperkinetically drawn to it perhaps!

He walked inside and glanced at the table where Richter would lay next time. He walked along next to the silent walkway and into the living room. He finds two dead dogs nearby. One of them was crushed underneath a landing pole, the chandelier light included and another one with a bullet in it's head. Blood everywhere, all over the place.

The basement door swings open and the killer jumps out through the open door and swings a baseball bat, hitting Lance square in the jaw, then another one in his right hand side, his shoulders swung down, then the bat hits him hard on the stomach knocking him down instantly.

Further back into town Tabitha stops slowly at a Quick Stop shop to get some gas in her car. As she

pays the cashier, Fred, she decided to ask him how well he knew the area and how long he stayed there.

He basically said, that he had been working there for about fifteen years, young at the most, he was about fifty-five years old then.

She asked him about a house at Lakewood Drive.

He started swearing about a vulture passing through putting delinquents to the test and admonishing the terrace with blood and guts and stuff. He then pardoned his misfailure to communicate and then swore on true testimony that there was a killer nearby. It hangs around these places for obscure misplacements.

Who is he, she asks.

He said, to be definitely truthful it's there to be reckoned by. It wants to hide. It means to fend for loyalties. And it's a mess. A logic with obscure strength to be reckoned with.

True that, she swore, and then questioned him again and got a reasonable difference without an honest answer to be reckoned for.

This man was abuse.

She handed him her business card, thanked him for his time, then she filled the gas tank, and drove off heading north.

Eric and Richter arrives at the house on 442 Lakewood. They trot up the front porch steps, and

Eric banged his hand against the door and yelled, "Hello! Is somebody in there?"

A pause. It was silent inside.

"Ready or not we're about to be! One, two, three!"

And BOOM!

Eric kicked the door open, he and Richter jumped through the front entry aiming their revolvers through in and through the doorway.

"Hey Richter, do you smell that?" Eric said.

"Yes it stinks."

"What does it smell like Ric?"

"Like old dead fish!"

"That's assuming you're personal. Now move it!" Eric screamed. "Come out here!" He raised a leg and kicked down the stairway door. And maggots, and leached came out.

"A corpse over here chief!" Said Richter.

"Two dead dogs!" Eric shouted. He looks back and sees a headless corpse laying flat on the back porch. "Shit! It's my old friend." The body of Tate.

Richter found a door to a recreation room. He kicked it in to find a pool table in the middle of a badly littered room.

"I found the light switch," Eric said, and he hit the power on.

They coughed and puked when the lights went on, it made them realize how much blood they were surrounded in.

Lots of gory head misplacements,

In the Buick outside, Lance woke up in the trunk and began to holler for help. "Heyyy, let me out of here."

Moments later, Tabitha pulled into the front way, and heard his screaming. She saved him by popping the trunk open with a crowbar she saw lying on the ground.

"Thanks, who are you?" Lance asked.

"I'm your fairy god mother, holy ghost," she said.

"Let's get out of here," Lance said.

"Eric! Detective Eric! Come out here, what are you doing?" Tabitha yelled.

Inside the house, in the pool room, a door busted open, making Richter and Eric flinch at the walking corpse of Amanda Reyes.

Richter unloaded six shots into her pussy, green globs of blood spattered out of her, then she had Richter stuck into the wall, where the killer behind it jammed a screwdriver through piercing Richter's skull.

"Richter!" Eric yelled. And he reached for the safety and plugged Amanda's walking dead body between the face and the thighs.

The killer dressed in black removed the screwdriver, letting Richter slide down the wall, leaving a bloody line smeared down the wall.

The killer in black steps behind Eric, and knocks him on the head with a club.

Lance jumps in and gets side whacked from the billy club.

Tabitha awkwardly jumps in the middle of the shooting match, but more hesitantly she did a better job at squabbling at the killer, because she managed to remove the black nylon mask off the killers head.

Her face looked just like Amanda, but it was a twin sister Natalie Walker.

Tabitha swung a deadly blow to the head and was knocked back with a forward hit from the killer lady.

Eric gets up and secures a headlock around Natalie's throat and bends her down between the knees and hits her hard to sustain the ability to fight!

A gun went off, it was Natalie, she managed to pull the trigger between her feet, and the bullet hit Lance in the guts.

Natalie reached away and brought back the screwdriver, tainted with blood, and jammed it in the middle of Eric's kneecap.

Eric screamed, and gleamed with torture in his thought process, hate and rage in the others.

Natalie rose quickly and stared at the handsome three with eyes of fire. And then...

Lance blows her away with a bullet straight in the forehead. He had Eric's gun in his right hand. He drops it, and then faints while saying, "Bitch!" with blood dripping between his lips.

"Rahhhhhh!" Screamed the walking corpse of Amanda.

Tabitha takes the gun, aims and fires, hitting the cadaver straight between the eyes. A green blood splatter. And then it falls backward, dying as it his concrete.

"There's two," Tabitha annointed with a smile.

The murderer is anything but the identical twin sister of Amanda, her foster parents were killed, she escaped and stalked and brutally killed her twin sister.

How did she reanimate her sister's corpse?

Lance is placed under care in the intensive laboratory.

Tabitha re-writes history with a new novel.

Eric pays a visit to Lance, walking by using a cane. He is alone.

"Hello Lance," Eric said.

Lance is asleep.

"All I want is to thank you for your dedicated work and heroic attempt at saving us one last chance to live. I want you to wake up, your nightmare is over. It's time to follow your dreams. Do you remember that talk we had about following your heart's desire? You just hang in there, man. We'll pull through this, and meet again when it's over..." Eric gasped.

A few days later, Eric stands before the grave of Lance, in the cemetery on a rainy stormy day.

Eric has a reoccurring dream while standing before the grave with his hat in his hand, as if he were saying the "Pledge of Allegiance." In his eye, he sees a sudden flashback of Lance standing in his garage, examining the Hugger bike, and Tate looking down and chuckling in a fond memory, Tabitha bringing him forth the kiss to his face, and finally the stagnant pool water in Amanda's backyard.

Eric looks up and sees a mirage of Natalie Walker in the distance dressed in black. He stares at without blinking, he doesn't even bother to draw his gun, and watches her as she eventually fades away and disappears for good.

Eric drops his employee badge onto the gravestone, along with some flowers, he puts his hat back on, and walks away, leaving the scene for good...

THE END

CRYPTOGRAM

PART 2: VICE VERSA

CHAPTER 1

It was a dark day and the night was soft. Evil perhaps. And demented.

A scrawny man in biker leather storms through the rough terrains with a shovel and a flashlight. He refers to himself as G. Funk Daddy. Something wicked. A man who has fetishes above and beyond danger. With him, a punk name R&B. Both men were Caucasian. Dressed in street clothes. They look like a couple of hillbilly rockers of the modern day.

G. Funk Daddy had long blond hair. R&B the same.

They walk behind an open field, somewhere over the canyons. We call this place Napalm Valley of the Southern California region.

The night grew dark and cold, and their walk continued for over an hour.

The two men are in their twenties, still in high school, somewhat dorky, yet they walk with precaution, and look as if they were on duty, like they owned the place. Self-imposing themselves like they are self-elite individuals, like prison guards on duty.

They come to a stop at the point of being in front of an undug grave. A casket that was stolen from the cemetery and planted here above ground, right here in the dirt.

R&B said, "Quick, give me the shovel."

G. Funk Daddy loosens the backpack straps and promptly hands over a bag with the shovel and a pick axe.

R&B swears to god that this is the mother's corpse.

"Who exactly are we watching here?" Asked G. Funk Daddy.

"The dead mother of our new classmate, Amanda Reyes."

R&B swings the axe and breaks the casket open. The stink from inside it makes the two wince.

R&B quickly revived it open. "Hand me the paper."

G. Funk Daddy unfolded a pocket book and hands him the paper.

R&B says aloud, "Here to fore, and each to his claim, arise my wannabe, arise!"

The dried corpse of Amanda Reyes begins to twitch and turn.

R&B recited, "Here to fore in which he claims stagger my brutal wife, stagger before me now!"

The corpse opened its red, white, and blue eyes and then sits up with a bone crunching rise. The clothing and crusty skin on the corpses back peels off as it bends forward and reaches its boney limbs aforth.

G. Funk Daddy spins around and falls onto his hands and knees, while vomiting, and quickly revives and offshoots the way he came with R&B himself. And corpse captures him and revives a mouth to orgy finger licking good appraisal.

The corpse French kisses G. Funk Daddy and here comes the tears of pain, survival, then the maggots, and puke!

Daniel wakes up from the bad dream.

Alone in the dark. About 5:30AM.

At least I'm up early, he thought.

It felt good to be awake now, because today is his first day of class at Will Wood High. He will be a senior this year. The past three exotic years he had been studying independently. He felt the time is near to complete the studying at a regular school.

Now, it's time to wash up at the basin, floss and then brush then rinse.

Before leaving the house he spent some time having breakfast, and idled to the framed picture portrait of his mother Amanda Reyes who had been dead and gone for seventeen years.

And then he locked the front door and headed off to school.

A long trip for the police to locate a section of missing grave. They flew out into the open airfields while riding in a Bell 206 helicopter, somewhere near a common ghetto. About a minute and a half trip, a great mile and half long walking distance for the men on foot.

"I've got it," Carter said. "I'm enforcing a land."

The pilot lowers the craft, the rotors skimming the surface, blowing dust in the mid October day sky.

They found a filthy rotten empty casket abandoned in an old slum yard. And it's inhabitance are missing.

In class, at Will Wood High, Mr. Mansua's Math Class, sat bunch of students seated in desks, four rows of six. They party when they're available!

They spat and chewed gum and screamed at each other. And then they renewed for the sake of agreement at the prize to be won by. A teacher agreed to be there where sat homicidal maniacs waiting to do the doing at focusing attention at the most who fuck around during class hours like calling their teacher a Mistress instead of Mister. They enforce the law a bit too much in this room. They pervert each other during normal business days.

In came in Mr. Mansua, and then next thing you know they become quiet, alert, not a whisper. Fuck ebonicks for now.

Everyone supports a theory now and then; that there is hope for survivalism and for the mentality that grows every now and then.

Once upon a homeless type there have been many reports of evidence about a groupie that never was alive. Here to be all in all the report to a new one again. Fresh reports serve better than the individual who climbs them. To the last second thought, who advises them? Bad people did and bad people now surrender to the source.

Every now and then there hears an oath and promise that here lies a corpse, and everyone's invited there. Once a hint always a hint.

A hidden legacy goes to show us now that we hint alloy. The metal shapes and sounds like a bat cave here. Put these away, all that we have is separate minds at work here.

So now all we have got is bad people behave a certain way. And we have those that behave alot better. And what do we get? A power struggle.

"Hello class," Mr. Mansua said. "Everyone take your chairs, now listen, we have a new student in class and his name is Daniel Jacobson. Everyone, give him some classroom effort and cheer."

Everyone claps together. Especially the girls.

It was a beginning to be.

"Daniel, welcome to Will Wood High," said Mr. Mansua.

"Thank you," Daniel said.

It's a good welcome day, he said to his class.

Daniel took his assigned seat.

G. Funk Daddy sat across from him, looking at Daniel a cursed expression.

"Class, we're going to start with bonus. Sherrie, would you please pass out Exhibit Book A."---- Sherrie walks in single file and passes out Math Books. Exhibit A's.---

"While we begin everyone move your chairs, and form into study groups. That is four persons in each group," Mr. Mansua said.

The class pushed their desks together forming six groups with four people at each.

The day went on well, and good it was. The day came and went so fast that it always should.

A careful start.

One more thing.

"My names Gary, what's up. Some call me G. Funk Daddy." He smiled.

Daniel said, "Hello. I'm delighted."

"Do you remember me in middle school? I used to pick on you in seventh grade," Gary said, exhaling a solid laugh.

Daniel cringed, not because of the memory of being bullied by Gary, it was the awful smell. He couldn't tell if it was Gary's breath, or something stuck to the bottom of his shoes. It was a dead fish stink mixed with vanilla miles.

Daniel stared at Gary, and had a visual hallucination of warts popping out of Gary's head, his tongue hanging down past his chin, puss boiling and spraying from his nose, and his eyes turning red.

Daniel shook in his seat and vomited on the floor.

Mr. Mansua stepped up and asked, "Are you okay?"

Daniel looked devastated and humiliated.

"Get your backpack and go see the nurse, you are done for the day, Daniel," Mr. Mansua suggested.

Daniel was told to stay at home.

His mother's grave had been reported stolen, and the casket has been revived, but the body is missing. And his foster mother didn't want to be the one to tell him. Not yet.

Daniel's foster parents were spoken to by the police.

Later they planned to take Daniel out to dinner, make him feel better, and see if there was anything they can do for him.

CHAPTER 2

Gary (G. Funk Daddy) beared a summer school ordeal when he went away one summer on a camping trip, and seeing twice the corpse of Amanda Reyes and, he became infrequently obsessed over the Amanda girl twice one day. He jacked up the frequency one day twice and further sold his life for an occasion of liking his meat stepped on twice the time expected to be an elsewhere individual, He had raped a corpse behind an elm school tree house. He could not help himself. Now that finished the favor. Let's just let them go for a while. End that favor. Dish.

Tonight, he lie there in bed just soaking it, and found a right girl just beckoning for deployment. At first he was only there part time. And the next he could be someone employed by them.

"Get back, lunatics!" he said. "And go!" He did.

He unintentionally drew a revolver with his lips and made a "U" shape and fired an assault grenade then he withdrew and pulled a fork out of the subterranean vessel and out the blow he took over the head.

He blooded up and out of the heredity of the man and carried his cadaver across the way over to the avenue, and guess what?

HE is a sick fucking lunatic. Now he rapes a corpse again, and again, and again.

The night had been desperate and dark past them days beforehand and blood all the merrier. Blood lust!

Blood had been gone and dead forever. No one will see this now except for you now Charlie Hustle!

About four weeks before Senior Year, Gary spent a lot of time chatting with classmates on the computer, and having private sittings watching videos and looking at pictures.

Later afternoon, a boring Sunday, Gary spent the day reading student profiles, learning all about secrets of his fellow classmates.

He sat there, heart pounding with paranoia.

If his dad catches him stalking someone he would have his ass for dinner. Gary was always afraid of his old man.

One night, he was caught sneaking his booze out in the backyard and he couldn't get over how badly he beat him that time.

All of this paranoid mind games made Gary want to puke, and the taste of vomit in his mouth gave him a thirst for blood and revenge.

On the computer he discovered an interesting blog about classmates and soon discovered the myth that a secret is being kept and it interpreted that the high school average classmate seeks revenge for father meets mom. And one of these states that a fellow student had a no mom or dad. It was Daniel Jacobson.

Boom!

This was four weeks before class started. Before Daniel's first day at school.

Gary had gotten obsessed with the dead mother. Danny surviving his mother's murder while in utero sounded powerful. It made him believe he could resurrect god from the tomb by raping her corpse.

No wonder Daniel puked his first day of school, while talking to Gary. Sickening!

It was Thursday, while Jacob headed for Gym class. He walked with Erica Cartwright, she was his English class partner, and today they had to study for a test while reading William Shakespeare's

Romeo and Juliet. And they were set to meet in the High School Library after Gym class.

Gary stood by at his locker reading the two of them as they walked and talked. He felt the urge to break them up and interrogate on their conversation.

Daniel and Erica set up a time and day to meet up at the school library and cram for a exam about Shakespeare. They said their goodbyes and split up, she headed for Art class as Daniel headed off to Gym class.

Gary who had been spying on them for a minute ran up to Danny and slapped him on the back and yelled, "Hi Dan, how's it going?"

Daniel smirked at him, "Hey Gary, how are you?"

"I'm good," Gary said, with a hunky dory approach. "Look man, we got to get to know each other better. My friends and I are planning a party. Do you drink?"

"No, I do not," Daniel said.

"Good! You get to be my D.D." Gary shouted.

"D.D.?"

"Our designated driver. You can drive us home after we get wasted," Gary said.

"No, I don't think so," Daniel said, thinking Gary was up to something.

"C'mon, I'll pay you. It's my bargaining," Gary said, aloud.

Daniel thought about it some more, and then nods, "Okay, what day do you prefer?"

"Tomorrow night. Friday. Thank god it's Friday. Ya' know TGIF," said Gary.

Suddenly everyone standing around them began to chant, "TGIF, TGIF, TGIF!"

Daniel looked around. This is one polite HELLO!

Gary and Daniel texted each other their phone numbers.

Gary smiled, "Okay, I'll shoot you a text."

"See you in Gym class, buddy," Daniel said, walking through the hall.

The class sat in category and did their drills, startle, stretch the hamstrings, butterflies, and push ups, while the teacher counted aloud to twenty.

"This is bullshit," a student murmured.

The Gym teacher hollered something about divided the class into two teams for Volleyball, while he marched around his students. And then he came to Gary, and looked at him hard in the rear and shouted, "Is it warm enough for you Gary?" Indicating that he is overdressed. Wearing gray sweatpants, and a gray woolen sweater. He was hiding something big time.

After that, the classroom divided into two teams, and played Volleyball in the auditorium.

Best of all, Danny scored thirty points in a row as he served for his teammates.

Gary pretended to not be so obvious being jealous. He would smirk and yell, "Whoopie!" At every move. But honestly, how couldn't you tell that Daniel was a smart kid, and great at everything he did.

After Gym class, they were in the locker room. Daniel couldn't help to notice that Gary's midsection was all covered in bumps, rashes and bruises. So that's why he's overdressed.

After lunch, Daniel and Erica sit tight studying and practicing for the quiz based on Shakespeare.

Daniel reads a study sheet that he had made during class, "Here is a two part question. Number one: When was William Shakespeare born, and here is number two: where was he born?"

Erica focused, cringed and then twitched in her chair, and she yelled, "1564 in Strattonford."

"No, no, no. It's Stratford-Upon-Avon. You got the year right. It was 1564. Can you guess what month?"

She frowned.

"Think about the Easter Bunny. Think about Fools Day," Daniel twitched an eye to her.

"April..."

"You got it," Daniel said, frowning. "Now I have another question, it's a bonus one. A: What, and where did Shakespeare build his theatre? B: What was it's name?"

"The globe." She smiled. "And I think it was in Southwark."

Daniel felt a breathtaking sigh, "You are amazing."

"I have a good study partner. You ought to be class president. You read like excellent," Erica said.

"It takes a full draft and an empty body. Sure read and ready for final print," Daniel said.

They are being watched by Gary who sat in a dark corner of the room, festering over how great he is, yet he had a fucked up birth. Gary couldn't get over how Danny managed to survive while his mother was stabbed and bled to death while being in her uterus. He grabbed an old yearbook from eighteen years ago, sat down and stared at the class pictures of Amanda, and Lance.

After a while of studying, Daniel and Erica put their pens and papers in their backpacks and left the library in peace.

Gary also knows that Daniel had seen his bruises and blisters. The disease he has from his nasty habits. He fucked a dead body.

Daniel drove home in his newly bought Honda Civic. A 1993. A used newly bought. It had lots of good mileage. His step uncle was a genius with cars and he had his own shop. He can soup up any automobile any day.

He drove home casually thinking, That Gary sure is weird ain't he? But you may never know. He is a new friend. And he could both be super spectacular, and maybe even wholesomeness in disguise. We'll have to wait and see about how Friday night goes. Then we decide if we'll have him over for dinner.

He then began to think about Erica and their homework assignment they had to do. An exam loaded with twenty-five questions about William Shakespeare.

He then feels flooded by the after exaction about the pragmatist involved here. He then suddenly realized there was a misrepresentation between them and the gang. And why Gary was so punked with about staying in school so late that evening. Was he serious? Or gay? And what were those god awful messy sparks of flesh beneath his pants? What did he do? It couldn't be sure, yet. He might have gotten herpes. Or it could have been an accident at birth. But he acted awfully virtuous beneath them jeans. It reminded Daniel of a circus actor that was used to the blame and felt righteous beneath his own strange oddly attractive being. But Gary truly ain't that clean. He wants me to drive him home right after the party. Daniel almost called it quits there.

Gary was at home in the workshed behind his house. He was assembling a few items in a coach bag. Rifle, shovel, and a crowbar. And then he filled half of a fuel tank full of gas.

He suddenly felt strange, as if something were gaining on him. Something cold like a ghost. It made him shiver. And then that's when the ghost came. It said, "Gary!"

It's voice echoed through the air.

He turned around slowly and saw darkness. No light.

"Gary? What have you done?" The ghost of a woman asked him.

Gary saw the face of a decaying dead woman.

"You want to play hide and seek?" Said the dead woman.

Gary closed his eyes and held his breath and quietly counted to three.

The dead woman grinned and said, "Let's share a romantic evening down at the cemetery.

Gary grinned, "Okay. Let's have it."

The dead woman said, "Come catch me if you can?"

Gary got aroused and felt like getting laid. So he put his tools aside and made a run for the cemetery. He drove his car and went to the Clear Ways Cemetery. It was way off road from the town and, people usually go out there to die. Nobody will catch him out there when he's bucking off one of the cadavers.

When he arrived at the cemetery he made necessarily sure that no one was there. And no one else was watching.

He used a crowbar to crank the caskets open and then he immersed himself to the

cadaver. The dead body of Amanda Reyes.

CHAPTER

3

The rest of that day felt entirely phoney. Gary was out having a brawl at the old covenant that no longer played rescue and now it's time for Daniel to support his weakness by having a brawl with the old technician. The keyboards on his steering wheel had a moment of collapse and now it's his Uncles tires that needed fixing. He had an accident while pulling into the curb. He ran over a fork.

"Aw damn it," he said aloud.

He had it fixed today.

But before that occurred he heard a shout from down the road. He could barely hear it. It sounded like a man shouting, "Don't go to party!"

He paid no attention. He quickly urged his call to his Uncle later that day. And while the tire and steering wheel were being fixed he quickly assembled a few products before school tomorrow.

He had his notes for the Shakespeare test, and he quickly glanced at the kitchen for a few things. He looked around for some ingredients and jotted down a few items he needed to get at the grocery store. It's his foster mother's birthday this week and he decided to make a cake for her and surprise her with a present and a card that said I LOVE YOU MOM. HAPPY BIRTHDAY.

The house was quiet. Peaceful. But there were no birds outside. Could that mean danger?

He glanced around the kitchen to find something to do. Maybe tidy up the mess, take out the trash, and adjust the heating console to make the perfect temperature.

He tried to keep himself alert, and keep himself busy while he waited for his Uncle to call him back.

"What is there to do?" He said.

Nothing.

So he sorted through his book bag. There is going to be a test next week. So what could there possibly be to do? He organized his notes and personal study sheets for Erica.

The rest of the day was quiet, gloomy and dark. It was getting cold outside. It was almost Halloween.

Daniel kept focusing on tasks until his car was fixed.

Gary climbed out of the grave, closed it, and limped up the steep cliff back to his car. He didn't feel up to going home. He does not want to put up with Dad banging his fist against his chest. She he tidied up and took a drive back home. A slow relaxed calm drive back to his home. And when he got home he sneaked around the side gate, and into the backyard and went back to the work shed.

While he was there he double checked his arsenal and made sure everything was there nice and neat.

And that's when the voices came again...

"Gary? Gary? It's time to make love again!" The ghost woman said, once more.

He turned around and saw three more virtual dead girls striving him off for some more corpse action. He then began to couch and hiccup.

"Gary? I'm waiting for you," she said.

And then three more dead girls from the past stepped out of the shadows in the night and reached out for him.

He fell to the ground and then grabbed an empty water pale and began puking mucous. A stream of red snot poured from his face, and he puked and puked until the bucket was nearly full.

The dead girls laughed and their laughter echoed making his head spin in wild vertigo.

That's when the bucket of puke began to drizzle hard, then it multiplied in shape and size. It began to overflow and pulsate like The Blob.

The puke and snot reached out from inside the pale and grabbed him by the throad and then he screamed, "Stop it please!"

Then the puke went away and the dead girls disappeared.

Gary stood up straight and patted himself left and right and tried to calm himself down after that lethal frightmare!

When he went inside his alcoholic father lain on the couch snoring. Gary slipped past him and went upstairs to his room and snuck a shower and soaked his sores momentarily and then he went to bed and took a nap.

That night, Daniel had a dream that he was in the high school auditorium which was also the basketball court, and the gymnasium where he played volleyball for physical education class.

He was walking around yelling, "Hello? Is anyone there?"

He heard Erica say, "Help me."

Then a volleyball bounced on the hard floor and rolled at his feet leaving a trail of blood. And then a fire erupted. The school grounds are on fire.

He heard Erica scream, "Help me Danny!"

Then he woke up catching his breath.

Then the next day at school Daniel did the usual course of the day. He went to his classes and studied with Erica in the school hall library.

She winked at him while they went over their study sheets.

Daniel pretended not to notice. And when it was time to go home for the day and enjoy the weekend off Erica surprised Daniel with a kiss on the cheek.

That made him soft and happy.

She said, "See ya."

And Daniel was enthused and happy to be around her.

Tonight he had promised to go to the party where the guys are gonna slam a few drinks, and drive them home.

Erica is not going to be at this party.

But he is a man of his word. He will drive his drunken classmates home tonight. He thought about calling her later though.

He waited around after school was over to meet up with Gary. He got his home address, and the appropriate time to pick him up.

"That night is going to be a bang!" he said.

That night Daniel shaved, showered and put on his best coat for the night. The frost air might chill beyond his actual goingness.

YEAH!

CHAPTER 4

Daniel took the drive across the city to pick up Gary and his partner guy friend R&B. That's what they called him. R&B and G. Funk Daddy.

The two of them were already hyped up and amplified for the party. R&B asked Daniel if he did any drugs and Daniel said, "No I don't I'm afraid."

These guys smell horrible, Daniel thought.

It was a scenic drive. It took about ten minutes to reach the road where the house party had been thrown.

Daniel parked it along the curb.

"Alright we're there, let's volminous!" Gary said.

They walked up the stretch of road to a wild night party being thrown.

This place is huge.

The house was extremely big. And everybody there were the big high school jocks. The girls were pretty. And everyone there said, "Hello" to each other.

The kitchen was full of geeks playing games on their cellphones, the pantry was being looted. Near the kitchen fridge there was a wild geek chase and some girl nervously serving them Jell-O shots.

Two seniors had chug-o-thons on the backyard swimming pool deck, and a large group of teens, a few of them were high school football majors naked in the hot tub with senior cheerleaders.

This place is packed beyond all means, Daniel said under this breath.

He heard wild sex thumping from upstairs.

Oh shit, Daniel said under his breath.

He took a deep breath in this humid, stuffy, warm air.

In a sense he would be glad to be here right now, but he kind of felt the urge to call up Erica and see if she would like to go out tonight. It would be nice to spend the night with someone beautiful and cuddly. But he was here on practical matters. To make sure the big jocks don't get sick and get his guys home safely. If he weren't here they'd have to sleep the night away here on the front porch. But like a man of his word he will drive them home safely. That means no drinking. He wasn't an alcoholic anyway.

Everybody is getting hammered.

Music playing the popular songs you hear everyday on the radio. Bieber, Taylor Swift, Maroon 5, One Republic, Capitol Cities, Rihanna, A Great Big World. Upstairs he could of swore he heard the new Megadeth being played aloud on huge stereo speakers.

Daniel marched briefly into the kitchen and asked if he can grab a soda.

He came back to the living room with a Schweppes Tonic Water. It tasted like an lemon pill.

"Hey, are you Daniel Jacobson?" Asked a party goer.

"Right, and you are Justin?" Daniel asked.

"Yeah. Who invited you?"

"I'm D.D. for Gary and R.&B." Daniel said.

"What the hell are you drinking that Schweppes for?

"I don't know either. I hope this ain't toxic."

"You can have some Jell-O shots at the kitchen bar."

"I would rather not, I'm designated driver for tonight," Daniel said.

"It's cool man, you can chill here. You can spend the night. There's some girls upstairs. You can go bumping for the night," Justin yelled, trying to sound vocal over the noise.

Daniel swore he can smell somebody shitting their pants.

"Shit!" someone cried.

Daniel covered his mouth and grimaced and stepped out of the way of the party. He went outside and caught Gary and R&B lightly sipping some ale.

"Guys, are you okay?" Daniel said.

"Yeah. Daniel I hope you didn't drink," Gary said.

"No." Daniel said.

R&B was spazzing about a temporary dismay happening outside to one of the geeks outside.

"We're about ready to head out," Gary said, finishing off his drink. "I'm going to have a smoke and head out. Are you alright Daniel?"

Daniel nodded, happy to be going soon.

R&B sat his beer down and lit up a tree reefer.

Daniel enjoyed the fresh air and he sighed with relief. And later on he safely drove Gary and R&B home. He let them off at Gary's house and they thanked Daniel and went around the back to the workshed.

Daniel felt glazed as usual. He was glad to be home for the night. He cooled off at home. But as for Gary and R&B the night was not over yet. In fact it's going to get insanely bad before dawn.

And later that night Daniel had remembered his dream from the night before, the dream about the school lighting on fire.

Later that night G. Funk Daddy and R&B took the coach bag of arsenal and hiked up the mountain trail to the cemetery.

They came into the crypt where Amanda Reyes body was stashed.

Gary cranked the casket open with the crowbar.

R&B said, "Man, I thought we were gonna' burn those damn corpses."

"Not tonight my good boy, we're getting horny!" Gary said, the usual.

"Man I told you to leave it alone. I ain't having it," R&B yelled.

"I'm doing my chore," Gary sounded salute to the flag.

"What the fuck did you bring the gas for?" R&B wailed.

"I changed my mind," Gary yelled.

"The fuck you did, now let's burn the body and leave and don't ever come back," R&B screamed.

"You want to keep yapping and moaning then wait outside," Gary said.

R&B pulled out his revolver, "I'll shoot her! I'll shoot her in the god damn face!"

"Put the gun away," Gary said. After a minute of gawking at them he screamed, "Put it down!"

"I'll fuckin' pull this trigger," R&B yelled.

"No you won't!" Gary suggested.

"Take a good fuckin' look between your legs and that's the reason why you are dying," R&B squealed.

"I'm going to count to five and that means put it down!" Gary said.

"You're making yourself sick, zip up your fly and let's move out," R&B said.

"You're a pain in the ass"--- R&B shook his head--- "put the gun down so I can have my leisure."

R&B pulled the trigger and the bullet ricocheted off the casket and Gary danced backward stumbling of position.

"You are damn lucky that didn't hit her," Gary said.

"You need it man, you need to quit her," R&B said.

Gary pulled out his revolver and shot R&B in the throat. He fell on his side and bled to death suffocating on his bullet.

Gary closed the casket wall and picked up R&B and dragged him far off to the field.

Gary was extra careful not to leave any trails of blood behind, he had covered his tracks and made it to the car, he went back for his bag of arsenals, and packed up his things and hid R&B's bleeding corpse. He wrapped his body up good with a tarp. An old military tarp he stole from his old man's Navy sack stored up on the rafters in his garage.

He drove to the school grounds. The campus was black and clear. No sign of anyone.

He carried R&B's cadaver and propped him up on top of the school gymnasium. He poured gasoline all over R&B's corpse. Then made a trail of it all around the building and around the school walkway.

When he lit a torch and dropped it on the wet gas the flames raced in circles around the school gym, the flame chased the gasoline up the walls and caught a glow on top of the roof, burning the body, and setting 50% of the campus in ablaze.

The school is burning down.

No class for a year.

Every student received a phone call notifying them NO CLASS FOR A MONTH.

Everyone is happy.

Gary was never caught.

As for the rest of the students enjoy your anticipated new schedule.

Everybody was relieved to hear that school is out for rebuilding, even Daniel was. Everybody slept in and spent cool cozy mornings at home.

When Daniel awakened in the morning he was the only one home. He laid on his back in the living room, on the couch, and watched some late morning television.

What a relief, he thought.

Even though he loved school it wasn't the problem for him, and that's the excuse for enjoying

a whole day off-----and not just one day, but two whole weeks, and a possible stretch to two more weeks to a few months.

Later that day, Gary dressed in his leather motorbiking coat, grabbed his change, his receipt, keys, and his riding helmet and climbed out his window and escaped his house through the backyard fence.

He got on his motor bicycle and jump started, released the catch, and drove on over to his friend's house.

Drinking for pleasure.

Trying to keep busy to dodge the suspects list about the school fire, his best friend that went down in flames, and keeping his distance from his mean miserable old man back at home.

And he is on the constant binge to soak his sores and keep people from noticing his paranoid complex, and his secret vomiting ritual.

People have got to learn someday, because murky is a disability being. An evidential recovering can span it's host in multiple platforms while being excused by people who laugh at each other and some will wait to see how better things could be if only they loved someone else better than he did.

Jokes on Gary, people.

CHAPTER 5

Daniel spent the whole day doing chores. Sweeping and mopping the kitchen, vacuuming the stairs. He had a few hours to drive to the mall and pick up a Birthday Card for his mom. And he gathered all the ingredients to make her a birthday cake. And then he prepared the frosting, and the decorations he then received a phone call.

It was Erica.

"Hey you," he said. "What do you think about the extensive time off?"

She said, "It's good to relax again. It's almost like a summer vacation in overtime."

"Bet you didn't even study for that quiz you and I were betting on winning," Daniel smiled to the receiver.

"That's boring," Erica said.

"It's okay. We got plenty of time."

"Would you like to come over tonight? I got something to show you," Erica teased.

"Alright. Just give me a few minutes," Daniel said.

He finished the cake after another ten minutes.

He planted the cake on the kitchen table, and placed the birthday card right next to it. I LOVE YOU, MOM, it said.

It was about 5 P.M.

He turned the lights out, grabbed his jacket and got in the car and took a ride to Erica's house.

It was late, somewhere around 10 P.M.

Gary was at beer drinking party at a friend's house. They were some older friends that built and raced bikes. They were somewhat normal to him.

Bunch of guys with Harley Davidson jackets, beards, rocker tattoos, and hanged out with women that looked like luxury models.

The anxiety on his mind had something to do with needing to take a leak every forty-five minutes, and hoping the make up painted on his crotch wouldn't wear off---he doesn't want focus on his bruised blotchy genitals---he tried to hide them!

He sneaked away and walked outside into the loose gravel to take a silent puke.

He sat his beer bottle down on the ground, bent down, and quietly let out the vomit, letting the thick white snotty mass drizzle out between his open lips. The infection is spreading madly.

He vomits for a minute straight and then one of the girls approaches him, and says, "Hi Gary. Want to come over and play."

He looks up at her and tries to speak, but instead of words coming out, it was a big gray splash of puke which flowed freely from his mouth, and splashed her right in the face and she screams, "AHHHH! Oh my god!"

Daniel arrived at Erica's place. Her parents weren't home.

He came to the front door to find it open.

"Hello?" He yelled.

"Up here," Erica said.

Daniel walked up the stairs into her bedroom to find Erica sitting by the flower pot, in a kinky bath robe, while tying her hair back and she was wearing lip gloss.

"There's something I want to show you," she said.

Daniel agreed, and smiled at her.

Kissing, necking, and cuddling came next.

Gary had serious explaining to do so he jet leg boogied out of the place while riding his motorbike.

In his minds eye, he saw his life coming apart into bits and pieces. And he wants to take everybody down with him.

So, when he got home he didn't bother sneaking in through the backyard, and climbing in through his bedroom window. Instead, he mozied on through the front door.

His old man, Jack, woke right up and screamed, "Where the hell were you?"

"None of your business pee eyed brain!" Gary shrilled with lungs in full force.

"You sonofabitch, you've gone too far!" His dad jumped out of the chair and screamed at him with eyes of fire.

"Up yours you miserable old hoot!" Gary screamed back. And went right up the stairs.

"You've gone fuckin up since the day you came back from prison. And I know you burned down the school, and I know about your friends. And I also know about you and that damned graveyard too!" Jack said.

Gary stopped at ease. "You know?" Then he turned around and grimaced at his father. "You blew it since the day I got back here. Always blowing the jug, screaming at the top of your lungs. And then I hear that mom passed away. YOU have gone too far. Always sounding the horn. Gimme back my wallet, you BITCH!"

"Hold a sec. You have gone rich in that cunt since the modern homestead brought beginess. First of all you fucked up in school, and now you're drowning! Second of all you blew your savings account on a second hand thug worship group, and now you'll be charged for bread right out of your mercy until the sky turns black with solid gold. You burned down the school and now you're going back to jail. And your obviously gonna die from that poison in your blood. Well son, it's time to pay blood. You're finished!" Jack announces. He licked his lips and tried to swallow them back.

"You want to hold me until the police get here? Fine baby pig. But I've got one mercy after your soul and it ends in pay time. You get it? You die boy, you die? Get bent and out of probation. Now get!" Gary raised a knife, a pocket blade, and he lunged it right at his stepfather Jack and pierced the blade into the skin of his silky white skin and withdrew blood and capped him off with his revolver. Blood thickens jets right out of his ears and pierced went the blade right into dad's groin.

Gary stood still for a moment or two. He grinned and said, "I'm so sorry babe!" He laughed and grinned in unison.

When he looked up he saw the winking corpses of girls he had fucked. Their reflections in the mirror staring right back at him.

Daniel moaned, "Ooooohhh and Ahhhhhh."

He had some of the best sex that every boy could dream of.

He laid on his back next to Erica and smiled.

"Did I pass the test?" Erica smiled, twirling her fingers across his chest.

"It was good. May I have another?" He smiled.

"Of course, my parents won't be home until tomorrow."

He sighed in passion and pleasure.

Gary was on his bike. He didn't bother with wearing the helmet and as he took the road, with the wind blowing on his face, the skin began to crawl, like worms squirming through his veins. And a chunk of flesh beneath the surface of his cheek began to peel away and break apart and flip, flap, and flop like a flag, and then blew off like a leaflet in the wind, leaving behind a red gash.

He was heading back to the house wear his biker friends and wannabe thug friends were, where he had puked in the girls face.

When Daniel's Mom and Dad came home they were astonished by the cake, the card, and the present for Mom's birthday. They loved him for it.

"What an angel," his Mom sighed.

"Hey, where is he?" his Dad asked.

They hanged up their coats and by the time Daniel came home he found them at the living room table playing a game of Yahtzee.

He then spent some quality time with the folks and had a steak dinner, some dessert, and ceremoniously played the piano for them.

At Erica's home, she wept and slept in bed. Before napping she had a thought about becoming pregnant after sex with Daniel. She was alone. She wept tears of joy and cried herself to sleep on the living room sofa. And she dreamed of something imaginable.

She slept. But then on forth her mouth moved, whispering "Don't" and then she started breathing rapidly.

Within her closed eyes, she saw an opening between canvas and figure drawing.

In her dream she saw a man standing near a grave. It looked like an awning figure with blood on his head. The man is Lance Weston. A voice narrating the image said, "This is Lance, a father of treason. He is the boy who gave birth to a man who claimed his last chance as a man." Lance stands late in the day next to a cross made in the dirt. "This is Lance, a father of treason. His boy Daniel is about to rescue you from hidden grace. We are here to stop you from leaving this place. You are alone at your house. We are here to warn you to turn off the lights."

Then the message becomes clear and more direct.

"You are alone. You must not stay. Wake up, and call Daniel. You have twenty-nine minutes before a stalker reaches your front door step. Wake up and call Daniel!"

Erica awakens gasping for breath.

She immediately got up and called Daniel. She needed him badly. He said, "Okay, I'm coming over to pick you up, and you can stay with me, here, at home."

CHAPTER 6

The party ended early, down at the big house near the vineyards, a long drive through the country. It is night. Five people left. The girl Samantha rinsed off her face, "I cannot believe he puked in my face like that," she screamed.

Gary's friend Robin tried to defend him, "He honestly did not mean to do it," he said, about her being made up to believe that his chicken means cow.

Ronnie Goldsmith, an ex-biker, keeled over and threw down a moistened towel and yelled, "Shit, he doesn't mean anything clever either."

"Just chill, Ron man, believe it. There's nothing wrong with you, me, and him," Robin trusted men. But he gave a rat's ass about clothing, so I'm him, he meant.

"When's he coming back? Do you know?" Ron the man said.

"I believe he's a coward somewhere. And there's nothing wrong here," Robin played games this way.

"Why don't you call him up?" Ron man suggested.

Samantha sat down, "Look, you want him over, then fine! I won't be it!"

"Just reason with him?" Ron the man said.

Robin went upstairs where Alicia slept. Their boy Boomer, a comedy guy, sat downstairs on the kitchen floor, making something to eat.

"Yo mister, I got caught up stealing the lettuce, I wanna play ketchup tomatoe (pronouncing it "Toematah").

"I believe it man, I really do," Robin smiled, as he had gone upstairs to visit Alicia.

Someplace, down the road, near the house Gary was on his way back, riding his motorbike. He's in the dark, coming for them, with violence, and ready to take them down to the ground.

Ronnie came outside, started his bike, and went up road. He was going out for a lone bike ride out in the mountains, for peace and tranquility.

He could have sworn Cheetah, their pet Chihuahua, had wandered astray down the road. So he revved up his motorbike, warmed up the engine, and started to head out down the road.

There was a long stretch of land caked between the house and the main valley park drive.

Down the road, Gary had sliced and diced Cheetah, their pet Chihuahua. He slit its throat, and sliced down it's gut, killing it fast. It's yellow fur all dust, and blood.

Down came the rain, as Ron came over on his bike. But at first he couldn't see Gary, because he's wearing all black leather, blending in with the darkness like a dream chameleon.

Gary pulled out his pistol, aimed it dead at Ronnie, pulled the trigger and boom! He shot Ron straight in the chest.

Ron fell backwards off his bike, and the bike kept rolling until it hit a tree and pop! The bike was split in two halves.

Samantha went outside, she could of swore she heard the roar of the bike, and the crash nearside the open road.

"Cheetah?" She called, but the dog did not answer. "Cheetah?" She said, again.

Samantha grew worried, and went and got a flashlight and went out to look for the dog herself.

"Cheetah? Come here boy."

Gary was somewhere close.

Samantha had no clue what was about to happen.

Gary tossed the dead pet at Samantha, it hit the side wall of the house, and left a splat of blood on the fence.

Samantha screamed, "Cheetah!"

The dog was torn to shreds.

Gary quickly ran up behind Samantha, covered her mouth, and stabbed her deep down inside her stomach. Blood gushed from her mouth, and body.

Boomer sat on the kitchen floor devouring a raw tomatoe. Buzzing with the munchies after a pot smoking session.

Gary slowly, silently, entered the house from the front door. He held an axe.

Boomer paid no attention, he sat with his back turned.

Gary stepped into the kitchen, getting closer, lifts the axe blade, and then swings it down, splitting Boomer's skull, and letting go of hostility. His blood showered the kitchen cabinets, and down he went.

Gary climbed up the stairway, heading for the shower, where he hid for about a minute. He made no sounds.

Somewhere on the upstairs level, Robin and Alicia were there, and Gary couldn't prove a thing until he got them.

He heard the sound of a thump, like somebody removing his boots and then dropping them on the floor.

He couldn't tell which room they were in. So he went back down stairs and marched into the play room. He searched for something fusible and uncovered a few fragrance candles. He walked back to the kitchen and turned on the gas stove then he lit the two candles and placed one the stairway, and the second one in the pool table room.

He then walked quickly outside and waited for commotion to stir up.

Six minutes went past, the gas stove fumigates the lower half of the two story brick house.

A moment of confusion happened when he heard the fire alarm turn on.

From outdoors Gary could specify a medium heat wave transactioning the place. He saw a retro stove flame from outside. Through the frontside window, Gary could see a blaze forming, and developing into a windstorm hurricane.

Boom!

Flames erupted, although, the house still stood their half in smoke and flames.

Upstairs, Robin and Alicia could be seen leaving their room. It looks like their taking off from the back door exit.

Gary smokes a tad bit of the farm by AC/DC lightning strikes.

The house blew up, taking down refugee wind and style with it.

He heard screams and he smiled.

CHAPTER 7

Daniel drove over to Erica's house to pick her up at home and take her back to his house for the night.

"Are you okay?" Daniel asked.

"Thanks for coming," Erica smiled.

She was dressed in Oscar the Grouch, bed clothes, wrapped up in a blanket, with sandals on. She immediately got in the car and they drove home to his.

They were glad to be near each other. Without hesitation they emerged together like the quickness of a clam door shutting instantly to avoid trespassers.

She told him she had a bad nightmare about an intruder coming to her doorway.

He asked her, was it the boogeyman?

She said, it was warning her to not stay home now that she was alone. It said something to do with a man and a burning stove. Decorates the trees with burning victims. A man who was the father of treason gave me a twenty-nine minute warning to call you and leave the house.

"Maybe it's got something to do with the school fire," Daniel said.

"Did you go to that party Friday night?" She asked.

"What? Yeah, as a matter of fact I did," Daniel said, full of surprise.

"What did you do?" Erica asked.

"I was a designated driver. Gary and his friend got drunk, and I drove them home," Daniel admitted.

"Sometimes I swear that you're a hidden locket. The school burns down and now nobody has the slightest clue. Now nobody can continue," Erica said.

"We're on the serving side, now with no proof," Daniel said. "I hate deceiving."

"Do you notice anything wrong? About Gary?" Erica said.

"To tell you the truth I puked in Math class, the first day I met him," Daniel said.

"That's the proof," Erica said.

Daniel frowned, he tried to think clearly. It was a tough thought, and his head was crammed with fear. "Well, he's definitely on something. I noticed... Um... He has problems. A virus. And incurable one."

Daniel remembered the day he saw Gary in the locker room, removing his pants, and he had blisters, welts, rashes, bruises, scarred tissue on his pelvis.

"Let's just drop it and enjoy the evening," Daniel said.

They went through the drive through and grabbed a couple of ice cream shakes.

The two of them went to Daniel's house, and enjoyed the rest of the evening. They sat down at the table, relaxed and spent an hour gossiping with his folks.

His mom fell in love for Danny and Erica.

He told mom that they are study partners in English class.

They were eager to know if the two of them were dating yet.

Erica told them a story about her dad who had worked as a book keeper, and became a property owner who owns six shopping squares in the valley, and her mother who was a violin teacher that now works part time at the public library.

Then suddenly Daniel received a phone call on his cellphone. It was Gary. He said that he needed his help. That his bike had broken down on the road somewhere near the vineyards. Daniel excused himself from the table.

"This won't take long," Daniel said. "I'm going to give Gary a ride home for now."

They told him to come back as soon as he's finished.

He said, "Don't worry, I'll be back."

Then he got in his car and journeyed off to meet Gary by the park somewhere out in the dark valley vineyards.

Someplace far away Gary was waiting patiently for the ride from Daniel.

Daniel was on his way.

The police were everywhere looking for Gary. First of all, they know he burned the school down. They are aware that he is on his bike someplace. They found his father dead in his house. They are searching for him all around the neighborhood.

His friend R&B was missing. His bones were found at the school.

Officers glanced around Gary's bedroom. They can see evidence of really sick behavior. It looked like a lair of a psychopath who was obsessed with death. Judging from the countless numbers of articles about dead hikers lost in the woods being tacked to the walls. A stack of yearbooks from years ago, some of the pictures were highlighted and bookmarked.

Out in the workshed on the side of the house, they see that he had been busy digging in the dirt. Shovels, rakes, hoes, a few crowbars, and a collection of knives.

They said, it looks like Gary has done some grave digging.

They found the bucket of puke.

They see soiled linen with blood and pus.

And they found make up. Something he uses to cover his scars and bruises.

There are some razor blades, and a mirror in the work bench. Empty bottles of beer. It shows that he's drinking and using.

What a disaster, they said.

Police combed the area asking for Gary AKA G. Funk Daddy.

The neighborhood Gary lived in was swampy. A nest of homes, two stories tall, old and decayed, built in the 70's, lots of luggage, and cargo crap strapped in the extra expense storage. Almost every house had old station wagons, and vans out of order. Lots of extra furniture and attics cramped with old style clothing's and furniture. The insides of the homes are cramped too. Swampy. Just plain old crap.

There was something about this night that kept people awake. Not fear, but awe inspiring wonder.

There is a clue somewhere that there is a ground breaking rule; it said, don't preach about it in yearbooks, don't mention it to someone. Just blow your head off cow curtain. It means: Blood Envy.

One man to look out for. The neighbors were not bothered by it. But someone is. The mother of Gary. She is in her tomb. Her ghost is waiting for him. She standing near the doorway of Gary's house where they had found his dead father.

This is leading to a future of syndrome.

Little did they know about Gary's corpse problem. Hanging out in the sewers drinking and barfing. Raping cadavers in the old abandoned cemetery. And killing his best friend and then burning down the school. And after killing his friends out in the forest. This is an amazing true murder case and it's going to change the world.

And now, Daniel is about ready to pick Gary up in the vineyards.

CHAPTER 8

At Danny's house, Erica is watching the news, she just heard about the manhunt; looking for Gary. Danny's in danger!

She let out a shrill cry.

His father got on the phone to call the Sherriff and Erica tried to call Danny on his cell phone.

It all happened in one big frenzy.

Daniel pulled up to the curb where Gary had stood waving his hand to him.

"Gary, what business do you have chugging a cold one out in the middle of deez woods?" He smiled.

"Hey Danny buddy. Thanks for pickin me up out in these woods."

"Hey, where's your car?" Daniel said.

Gary climbed in the passenger seat, and said, "I didn't have my car, I was on my bike."

"Where is it?" Daniel said.

"Sitting in the ditch down the road," Gary said.

"Which way?" Daniel asked, conservatively.

"What you don't believe me?" Gary said.

"No pun intended, dude. I mean you can't just leave your ride parked out in these woods like that," Daniel said.

"It's up the road. On the left hand side." Gary said.

Daniel got out of the car and walked up to the curb and saw a trashed motorbike. He looked off to the right side of the road and saw smoke, a burning house nearby, ten yards down the way.

"What is wrong?" Daniel whispered.

The car horn HONK!

Gary was in the driver's seat, Daniel walked back to the car.

"Get inside partner, I got something to show you," Gary said.

Daniel got in the passenger side and Gary began to drive further down the road.

"What's with that burning house dead up the road?" Daniel asked.

"Quit asking stupid questions," Gary said.

"I've got every right to know!" Daniel shouted.

"Calm down dude, and listen. I'm taking you for a drive through the forest to show you all the people

I killed," Gary insists. "Take a look to the left, and now to the right."

Daniel stared across the street and saw Samantha's bloody corpse tied to a tree.

"What the heck?" Daniel said.

Daniel looked to the left and saw Ronnie's cadaver hog tied to a stooping tree branch hanging closely above the street.

Daniel looked all around and saw Boomer's blood soaking corpse tied to a Deer Crossing Xing down the road.

"You want to know something Danny?" Gary put his foot to the brakes. "You don't give a lot, but I know something. Your mother is a girl who was murdered some time ago. And you were her offspring. She died with you in her. And you survived the brutal killing. And I absolutely love to play with her cadaver."

Daniel blinked a few times, "Why don't we go home?"

"It's no joke bro. Now listen to me, on the count to three I want you to get out and start to jog, and I'm taking your car and I'm leaving town."

"You're making a big fuss out of no mistake. C'mon, I will drive you home," Daniel remarked.

"Get out now dude," Gary said. "Or I will kill you."

Daniel got out. Took a few steps backward, and then turned around and ran for it.

Gary nodded and started to drive off.

Daniel got on his cellphone but before he could make the phone call to the cops it rang big time, it was Erica, trying to see if he was alright.

When he answered he told her what happened, and the cops were on their way, up the plaza somewhere next to the vineyards square, out in the boondocks.

Gary drove down the hills in the backroads and stopped by the cemetery where he and R&B always used to hang out.

He parked the car around the corner between the old graveyard and the ditch. He got out of the car went for a walk through several rows of graves.

He stopped at the bridge that crosses a creek and found a crowbar. He needed one. He stepped down a stoop and stopped before the grave of Amanda Reyes. He bent forward to crank the grave open but suddenly the grave door busted open and up came a cadaver back to life, dress in black, and it grabbed Gary by the crotch and slammed him up against wall, squeezing his balls making them crunch, and squish. And making all kinds of blood splatter up from his pelvis, and all over the place.

Blood gushed from his mouth, and blood sprayed in all directions.

Gary dies in misery and then the corpse went back to its grave, leaving Gary's corpse strewn across the cemetery floor. His spine bent backwards in half. His eyes open wide. His mouth wide open. Dead.

Daniel caught a glimpse of the burning house in ruins. The police were on their way. He was cold, tired, and afraid. His feet hurt, and his back had been feeling cramps.

For a brief moment Daniel saw himself suddenly surrounded elsewhere, in an entirely different location. It looked like an old sewer system with a house next to it. It seemed like a totally different day.

In the distance, he saw a woman dressed in a white gown coming towards him.

"Go ahead and live your life Danny. Mommy is watching," said the ghost of Amanda Reyes.

Daniel froze in anguish.

"You're safe now. Go home to your family," Amanda said.

Daniel started to cry. He quivered. He grew quiet and sad.

The ghost of his mother held him tight until help on the way came.

She disappeared when the police showed up.

An officer showed up, "Are you okay?"

"I'm fine."

Three more police cars arrived.

The continuing officer called for the fire patrol.

Daniel explained that a friend from school called him out here, and took his car and drove away.

The police gave him a lift to town and took him to his house where Erica and his folks are.

A day later, the following morning, they found Daniel's car at the cemetery, and Gary's cadaver laying still in the dirt out in the graveyard.

IN THE END

Daniel learned about his birth and who his original mother was, and the horrible murders that were committed by his aunt, the identical twin sister of his mother Amanda Reyes.

His life was always decent until the day he had heard this awful story about his life. And for the first time he felt an awful sense of dread and fear. He felt cold on the inside. He was negative, and irritable.

He even had a hard time swallowing this story about Gary and his habit of digging up his mother's corpse and necrophiling it.

He cried tears of dread, heartache, and pain.

He felt the loss of decency for the first time. It took him a while to stand up and continue his life.

All of this paranoia and fear had just started just when his life was getting good, and better, while dating a girl from school, Erica, and becoming a grown man.

He held on tight and tried to hold on.

He spent a moment alone. He showered, cried while he bathed.

And after a forethought of remembrance, he continued to do good in school, and he got even better when his relationships got even better with Erica, and he made a whole bunch of new friends.

And he was given a lot of money to continue his life and live happily ever after.

He was strong willed, and grew up to be millionaire, and he was happily married to Erica, by the time he reached the age twenty-one.

The story of Cryptogram and the terror about Gary and his dangerous habits and onslaught became a popular campfire tale and a school of wisdom and thought.

The End.

AUTHOR'S QUERY

I first wrote Cryptogram as a screenplay back in the Summer of 2002, I originally wanted to shoot it as a Horror Movie first.

I kept it all these years and decided to re-write it as a novel, and make a Part 2. Twice the story in one brand new package.

Part 2 is based on a mirage I once seen appear on my bedroom wall. It was the story in detail appearing like a movie being projected on a screen, and it's title said "Crypt 2." I remembered it vividly and wrote it down. This was about ten years ago when I saw this image take place. Sometimes vivid hallucinations occur like a movie to me.

To this day I would like to make movies based on both stories Cryptogram Part 1 & Part 2. Lots of plot twists with high body count, with lots of blood, and keeps moving.

This is scary.

I hope you enjoy it.

David Michael Medina
Folks and my friends call me Mike.
11:34 P.M. Sunday, February 24 2019
Pacific Standard Time.

Printed in the United States
By Bookmasters